MAGICAL PRACTICE

*Applying Magical Training
To Your Daily Life*

DRAJA MICKAHARIC

To order additional copies of this book, contact:
Xlibris Corporation
1-888-795-4274
www.Xlibris.com
Orders@Xlibris.com
19799

CONTENTS

INTRODUCTION

The study of magic is a continual, ongoing, and thoroughly fascinating affair. In one sense, magic means different things to everyone who studies the subject, as there are always differences in what each student is able to learn, even when they are studying with the same teacher. In the beginning of the study when all of the students are in the same class, striving to master the same basic material and exercises, there is a sense of community and yet a sense of individual uniqueness that I do not believe is matched in any other field of study.

As with many other groupings of people, some people come to the study of magic in an attempt to find a group of like-minded people to associate with. They are looking, whether they know it or not, for a social support group, one that will give them attention and at least a minimum amount of social affection, the necessary to all humans sense of belonging. As this is precisely the kind of thing that a real magical study group must discourage to be successful, these people are often disappointed, so they turn from the group after a few months or a year's membership.

In those cases where the people do not leave of their own accord, the instructor must find some way to discourage them, driving them away as it were. Of course, this is usually accomplished in such a way that the person leaving is very sure that they escaped the clutches of the foul beast heading the group by the very skin of their teeth. Thus, it comes about that serious magical groups, those that have no interest at all in being a social support group, quickly develop a rather negative reputation.

On the other hand, those groups which provide the social contact and support, personal attention, and the group affection, that their members require, as well as assuring the members that they have attained a particularly marvelous place in the universe through their membership in the group, tend to grow large and be well thought of, although they actually accomplish very little.

One of my own early teachers was disdainful of magical groups, because he said that any group with a good reputation was not worth belonging to, while any group with a bad reputation probably was either directly evil or a very serious group indeed. He further told me that since it was more than just moderately difficult to determine from the outside whether a group was either evil or just very serious about what they were doing, that it was the best policy to simply avoid them all.

Therefore, since I have been in practice in New York City, I have avoided associating myself with any of the many magical groups that are located here. On the other hand, I know of one group of ceremonial magicians who I consider not only excellent magicians, but also quite serious workers for the good of mankind. This is, however, only one of several ceremonial groups that I have learned are located in New York City. I have also heard this group being condemned for being 'snotty, exclusive, money hungry, sexually oriented, and being simply a social club.' Not being a member of the group, I cannot provide introductions, but I will say that I had been in New York City, actively looking for such occult groups for over ten years before I even heard rumors of their presence. The best occult and arcane groups do not ever advertise for, or even solicit, new members.

A Cuban client of mine once told me that New York was the home of the greatest collection of magical schools in the world. I can beleive this, although if I accept that proposition, I must say that Paris is probably home to the second greatest collection of magical training schools. In one apartment building that I know of on the upper west side of New York, there is a synagogue of Kabalistic Jewish Mystics, a Vodoun house, and a Santeria family. The apartment building also houses an Indian Guru, and several other religious practitioners, all of them teaching their arts esoteric to eager students.

That the practice of magic is so widespread in this modern computer age is something that is not at all well known to the average citizen. In my book *Magic Simplified*, I make the point that the exercises used to develop someone magically have many other uses in the daily life of the person using them. In this book, I hope to show what some of these many uses are. It is not necessary that a person become a magician to be able to master these exercises, as they are all exercises that lead to self-development and the expansion of the native abilities of the person practicing them. Awakening and mastering one's native abilities is certainly a worthy goal in itself. One need not go any further than this if desired. Of course, once these fundamental exercises have been mastered, it may well be that the individual may now wish to practice magic.

The application of these magical exercises being noted, I have added a few words concerning the making and using of magic mirrors. I believe that this will give the magician an excellent start in beginning their career, whether they wish to practice privately to their own advantage, which I recommend, or should they wish to engage in a more public practice for money. The effective use of a magic mirror is certainly the most efficient way to learn many things that would otherwise escape ones ken. I consider the mirror to be a most useful tool for a magician.

There is some rumor circulating that magicians and witches should not charge for their services. Those who do not wish to pay for value received have probably spread about this obviously false information. This rumor is patently false, as any work that is requested should always be paid for. This applies as directly to magical work as it does to house painting, the printing of letterheads, and doing the laundry. Only those who feel their work has no value should turn from accepting payment for it. On the other hand, as with everything else, the work should be priced in accordance with what the client feels it is worth, and in consideration of the out of pocket costs of the magician. For many years, I have made it a point to have the person requesting magical work pay me only when the work was completed to their satisfaction. I believe that this is a satisfactory solution to the problem faced by someone paying in advance for work whose outcome they may be in doubt of. In this way, if the person is not satisfied with the work, they need not pay. Over the years, I have found there to be no difficulty in collecting the agreed upon fee from those whom I have worked for.

In this regard, I generally allow the client to set their own price on the work I am to do for them. Naturally, this determines how much effort I will put into the work, as well as revealing how much interest the client has in actually having the work done. Occasionally, but rarely, I have done work for nothing. In almost all cases, this was in connection with clients who needed to advance themselves economically. I try to assure myself that all of my clients are working and earning a decent living. Should I hear that one of my students or clients is unemployed, I will usually do something to insure that they obtain a decent job as quickly as possible. Naturally, I do not ever attempt to interfere in other aspects of a client's life. However, I do believe that everyone should be employed and earning their own way in the world.

I hope that this rather rambling introduction answers some of the many questions posed to me by readers of my books over the years. I am no longer answering individual readers letters, although I do like to hear from those who enjoy my books.

Draja Mickaharic
February 2003

CHAPTER ONE

Relaxation As A Constant Practice In Life

As someone seriously interested in practicing magic, you are probably aware that the first exercise given to most students of the arcane arts is that of the relaxation of their physical body. This is probably one of the most important things that the new occult student learns, as it is the physical key to success in any later efforts in either concentration or meditation. Mastering relaxation of the physical body is an absolutely necessary first step to learning the important art of astral projection. There can be no doubt that relaxation of the physical body is something that every occult student must learn and master early on in their training.

Of all of the exercises given to the student of the magical arts, relaxation is the one exercise that is probably more productive of physical and health benefits than any other. The person who truly masters the art of relaxation, and continues to practice relaxation every day, long after they have mastered the exercise, will gain benefits in health as well as those which come from undertaking the study and practice of magic. Lower blood pressure and a more steady pulse are only two of these several benefits often reported.

Unfortunately, most students do not carry the lesson of relaxation very far into their daily life. The daily experience of living in the relaxed state can have even greater benefit for the student than it can provide them in their study of the arcane arts. Below are explained some of the ways in which extending the physical practice of relaxation to the everyday life of the student may be easily accomplished. The many advantages of living in a physically relaxed way are available to every person who practices relaxation, as well as to every student of magic or the occult sciences. All of these advantages may be discovered and successfully explored in your everyday life.

Seated Relaxation

Most people do not obtain the rest that they should when they are seated. They sit down supposedly to take a load off their feet, but they are still not usually sufficiently rested by sitting. This is because few people really relax their leg and back muscles when they sit. When they maintain these muscles in a state of tension while they are sitting, they devote physical energy to these muscles. By devoting physical energy to keeping these muscles tense, their body cannot gain the benefits of physical repose when they are in a seated position. A person who can sit down in a chair and really relax their muscles can obtain more rest in ten minutes than a person who cannot relax their muscles will be able to obtain in thirty minutes.

Anyone can learn to place themselves in the passive and relaxed state that the relaxation exercise encourages you to develop within yourself. Learning to enter that physical state is the real point of learning to relax all of the muscles of your physical body. Being relaxed in life will keep you from developing nervous tensions, and even keep you from developing many of those annoying nervous mannerisms that people rarely ever tell you that you have. Relaxation will also assist you in keeping your attention focused where you wish to place it, whether it is on your work or on some other matter.

In these days, when everyone seems to spend a certain amount of time each day sitting at a computer keyboard and staring at the screen, learning to relax yourself when seated has become of absolute importance in the life of most people. Relaxing yourself will mean that you will no longer feel stiff and cramped when your computer work session is finished. Sitting in a state of relaxation will also mean that because you have not used your physical energy keeping your muscles tense, you will have sufficient physical energy left to devote to other, and possibly more interesting, things. In fact, as you will have worked more efficiently when you are relaxed, you will now have both the time and energy to devote to those things that are more pleasant and beneficial to you, and to your personal development.

Whenever you are seated, whether it is at work, on a bus, at a restaurant, or at home, you should immediately begin consciously relaxing yourself. You may relax yourself by whatever method you are accustomed to using, but you should begin relaxing yourself as soon as you sit down. Once you are relaxed, you should impress upon yourself that it its your intention that you should always remain relaxed when you are seated.

Your sub conscious mind will be happy to remind you of any tendencies for your muscles to become tense again. This requires only that you pay some slight attention to your subconscious mind, by directing to it a small part of your being. The signal from your subconscious mind will tell your conscious mind to deliberately relax that part of your body that has become tense. You can direct that part of yourself to return to the relaxed sitting state, the state you may consciously assure yourself is so beneficial to you.

Ultimately, through practice, this simple process will become entirely automatic, and you will find that you can maintain yourself automatically in the relaxed state whenever you are seated. Once you have mastered maintaining the relaxed state, whether you are standing or seated, you will discover that you are considerably more rested at the end of your workday than you had been before you began the process of consciously relaxing yourself when you were seated.

Relaxing Yourself For Safety's Sake

One of the advantages of living your life in a state of complete physical relaxation is that you are less liable to injure yourself from the usual stress and strains that come onto any of us in our normal daily life. This can actually be a lifesaver, physically as well as mentally. Some years ago, during an ice storm I took what would have ordinarily have been a very serious fall. Because I was completely relaxed when I slipped, I fell much like a rag doll. As a result, I suffered no physical injuries at all.

That same ice storm brought a number of people to the emergency rooms of the cities hospitals, many of them with serious broken bones of every sort. Most of these fractures were due to falls on the ice like mine, or to even less serious slips and falls. The icy streets of the city were a trap for the unwary, and a very dangerous trap for those who were both tense and unwary. Unfortunately, these often seriously injured people were not physically relaxed when they lost their step, fell, and hit the icy ground. Bones in a tense person are covered by a solid muscle mass there is no soft and relaxed muscular padding around them to adsorb a blow. The relaxed person has their muscles held lose, in an open and relaxed state. These relaxed muscles act like padding, cushioning and adsorbing bumps and blows of any kind that may come to them.

You might test yourself occasionally on your ability to instantly release all of the tension from your body, collapsing to the floor like a rag doll. I would recommend a heavily carpeted floor for initially practicing trials of your abilities in instant relaxation. Once you master this art, you can fall comfortably on hard wooden floors, or even on concrete surfaces. This exercise is quite similar to one that people studying Ju-Jitsu practice. Once you have mastered this technique, you need never fear further slips or falls as either being hurtful to you, or unduly destructive of your physical body.

Ordinary slips and falls are a great hazard to the fragile bones of elderly people. Broken hips among the elderly are an almost daily hazard, especially for those who are past seventy. The process of living your life in a state of relaxation seems to be one way to rectify this potentially dangerous problem, regardless of your age.

Instant Relaxation

Instant relaxation, once you have mastered any of the ordinary techniques of relaxation, is only a matter of gaining experience through practice. It has the advantage that you can use the technique to gain quite a bit of real rest when you are traveling home from work on public conveyance such as the bus or subway. It is certainly an improvement over riding public transportation in the usual state of tension and nervous agitation that you will find in the average commuter.

Relaxation may also be used to rest and refresh yourself during or between the unending series of meetings that some companies sccm to specialize in. Being relaxed will give you a good edge of awareness over others who may be attending the same meetings. When you come to a meeting in a physically relaxed state, it seems that the information you need is more quickly available to you, being at the forefront of your mind as it were.

Relaxation For Habit Change

Whenever you are faced with something you know will be difficult to accomplish, such as breaking a bad habit, dieting, or quitting smoking, it will always go much better for you if you relax yourself every time the desire to break your resolution comes over you. Relaxation, often combined with a few deep breathes, will measurably improve the situation for you. I have found it beneficial to relax myself and take a few deep breaths every time I am faced with a desire to have a bit more to eat. In this way, I have managed to gain at least some control over my tendency to gain weight. Over the last few Christmas seasons, I managed to limit my weight gain, and to lose the gained weight by the middle of January. That is something of a record for me, although I am still hoping to lose the twenty or thirty some pounds I have managed to gain since I passed sixty.

As I have mentioned, mastering relaxation is the first step to learning any of the arcane arts. It is also an important step in mastering any kind of physical activity. As just one example, relaxation is one of the first lessons taught in any serious study of the martial arts. However, I believe that you should not only master the art of relaxation, I believe that you should apply physical relaxation as far as is possible in your daily life. For your own good, you should master the art of living a relaxed life to as great an extent as it is possible for you to do so.

CHAPTER TWO

Developing Personal Magnetism

Most People Ignore Life

A little reflection will show that people are by no means fully awake and attentive all of the times that they might otherwise seem to be. A latent, and usually unnoted, somnambulism is perhaps more common in humans that is complete physical wakefulness. Few facts are of such great importance as this observation in the interpretation of both the complexities of human social life, and the course of human history.

"The strangest fact that everywhere confronts the student of civilization is the amazing credulity of the majority of mankind. There seems to be no limit to what humankind is prepared to believe or accept. So eager has mankind been to swallow all forms of belief, that the human imagination does not seem to have been able to invent anything at all that is some place or another, at some time or another, has not passed for either absolute, or divine, truth.

"It is not ever a sufficient explanation of this phenomenon to say that human beings have such beliefs because they know no better. Indeed, this negative statement must be reinforced by a positive one. Men believed, not because they were ignorant, but because they were, are, and always have been, so made by their creator that they are dominated by ideas. Thus, mankind is dominated by foolish ideas if wise ideas do not seem to hold them. Mankind is dominated by absurd ideas, if more reasonable ideas, do not reach him. Ideas of some sort, or of some kind, always seize people emotionally. These ideas, whatever they may be, once attaching themselves to people, can utterly possess and dominate them.

"People can be talked into all sorts of beliefs. Absolutely nothing but contradictory experience prevents them from believing anything, and in most cases the mere having of contradictory experiences at some time in their lives is not sufficient to prevent them from falling into preposterous errors.

Ernest Carroll Moore, LL.B., Ph. D.
University of California, 1899

For most people, judging whether to believe someone or something will ultimately fall into a decision based on the person's prejudices alone. Most people are actually utterly incapable of judging anything by rational thought, regardless of what they may believe about themselves. Most people go through life as if they were asleep. As one author stated, when writing about psychic phenomena:

". . . My method for detecting frauds and charlatans does not depend so much on my great mind as the seat of my pants. The method in fact requires only a sentence—people who agree with me speak the truth, and those who disagree are frauds and charlatans."

This is not to say that other, more objective systems of judgment do not exist. However, even the best of these supposedly objective systems of judgments, are usually based on emotion driven and deeply accepted prejudices. The same author goes on to add:

> To some extent, I've learned that people are likely to believe what interest them, and disbelieve anything they find boring.
>
> Ron McRae
> "Mind Wars" p 131
> St. Martin's Press, New York 1984

How Do People React To Communications From Others?

With this in mind, it must be understood that people will first react to any communication they receive based not on the logic of the arguments, or the wit displayed by the communicator, but solely on the sub conscious reaction that they have to the person communicating to them. This reaction occurs because their emotion driven sub conscious mind always has greater influence over the actions and beliefs of any person than their conscious mind does. The sub conscious mind judges only based on the emotional prejudices and fixed emotion-laden beliefs that it has absorbed during its lifetime. The persons sub conscious mind will give these emotional beliefs and prejudices much more weight than any verbal information that it receives from the conscious and sub conscious communication it holds with any speaker.

> Understanding this one fact, the importance of emotions in communication, can make all of the difference in the world to you over the course of your life.

This fact explains why the successful communicator goes out of their way to present an acceptable personal image as well as a socially personable image to those with whom they are communicating. Realizing that they must first win over the person through their visual persona, their image, they do this as well as they can before preparing to win the person with their words. Naturally, the more personally magnetic and attractive their persona, the better they will be accepted by their listener.

Personal Magnetism

It is through your personal magnetism, your "ineffable unconscious charm" that you sway the opinions of others. The average person always holds any discussion or argument you may have with them or with another person, as secondary to the charm or magnetism that you display in putting forth that argument to them.

Therefore, if you wish to successfully sway others to your will, in any manner at all, it becomes imperative that you master the art of personal magnetism to as great an extent as it is possible for you to do so. It does not matter if you are a politician swaying the course of national affairs, or a fishmonger selling fish to housewives. In all instances, people will respond more quickly to your personal magnetism that they will to your verbal arguments, or to the logic of your rationally chosen words.

The true course of the affairs of this world is actually conducted by swaying the emotions of others. Those who control the emotions of others by their magnetic personality have always, and will always, rule over those following masses who are so eagerly and unconsciously swayed by the tune prepared for them by those charmers that these masses so eagerly follow.

Magnetizing Other People

In all societies, the masses have a preconception of what a leader is supposed to look like, and how a leader is supposed to act. The person who most closely matches this culturally defined image of the leader will be the one that is most successful in swaying the mind and hearts of others. The person who rebels against this image, and who insists on being the 'odd ball,' may have their moment, but the mass will always turn from them to the one who matches their cultural image of leadership in time.

In addition, it is necessary for the person who wishes to lead others to realize that people, almost all people, sincerely wish another person to lead them, although they will usually deny this if asked. The majority of people seek to surrender their personal autonomy to another person who will promise to take them to where they believe that they wish to go. However, the 'leader,' whom they willingly surrender to, always has his personal agenda. While the leader may direct his follower, or group of followers, in the direction they beleive they are going, there will come a time, when they have accepted enough of the leaders beliefs and discussions, that they are prepared to follow the leader to the destination he specifies, rather then to the one that they believed they originally desired to reach.

These comments concerning the nature of leadership must be recognized by anyone who sincerely wished to lead others. Leadership of any group for a short time is not impressive. Leadership for long periods is accomplished only through understanding the true nature of leadership.

Magnetizing Other People With Ideas

To magnetize people by your presence, or by the force of your personality, it is important that you first understand the power of ideas. You must realize that ideas, in their basic form as human thoughts, are always real forces in the universe. For example, it should be immediately obvious to you that only those thoughts that are in the mind of a person can ever be expressed or manifested in the physical world through actions. People have muscles so that they can act, but without the presence of thoughts or ideas, no physical actions are ever possible.

The thoughts that do not ever enter into a person's mind cannot ever be expressed through their actions. These unknown thoughts will never be actions, become words, or be anything else. Unknown thoughts cannot ever result in anything at all. If it is desired to motivate a person to follow a plan, or to accept a course of action, it is always first necessary to place the motivating idea, or ideas, into their mind.

The person who is constantly successful in placing ideas into the minds of others, and as a result is successful in motivating them, is a person who will be classed as a leader. This person, the natural or developed leader, the person who radiates magnetic charisma, is the one whom we refer to as someone who possesses personal magnetism. It is this kind of person, one who has fully developing whatever natural personal magnetism they were born with, that you should strive to become.

Requests for someone to follow a particular course of action may be placed into the mind of another person by anyone at all. Whether or not the person who receives them ever heeds these requests is another matter entirely. Requests for action are most often placed in the mind of another either through the process of a direct command, or through the process of a more gentle suggestion. Directly commanding another person to take any action usually results in their emotional prejudices against placing themselves under the command of another person automatically producing a mental counter command, or at the very least, a minor internal emotion driven mental rebellion.

In most cases, this emotion driven internal opposition to the command given them immediately arises within the mind of the person being commanded. The person's dislike of, or their resistance to, the real or imagined authority of the person commanding them may motivate this counter command. When the person commanding them is in a position of real or implied authority over the one commanded, this mental reluctance to obey the commanding person is usually overcome by the hearer's emotionally driven feelings of the necessity of their submitting to the commanding persons authority. In this case, those desired actions that were expected to follow, in accordance with the command that was given the person, usually occur. Thus, the command is obeyed, but its presence often engenders a degree of resentment in the person being commanded.

Most humans seem not to fully trust those people whose authority they have not consciously submitted themselves to in some way. Those people to whom they have surrendered themselves emotionally, on the other hand, most humans seem to trust absolutely. This surrender of personal autonomy, with or without emotional surrender, is usually the product of emotional conviction or of economic necessity. An example is the surrender of autonomy as it is found between an employer and an employee. However, the surrender or submission of one person to another person may also be the result of curiosity, applied moral authority, or even the weight of shear charisma on the part of the person being surrendered too.

A suggestion, especially when made by a person apparently possessing authority, brings no such immediate emotional opposition as would internally result from a direct command. The recipient of the suggested idea always seems to feel that they can either accept the suggestion given them, or reject the suggestion, as they desire. They usually believe that their following the suggested course of action, or abstaining from it, is always a matter of their free choice. The person being suggested to believes that they have maintained their prized free will, and that they continue to control the situation. The recipients ultimate acceptance or rejection of any suggested idea, as it may be proposed to them by the person making the suggestion, always has its real origin in the other, non physical, facets of the communication. Thus, there is usually not the strong surge of emotional opposition to a suggestion that is found in a direct command.

Of the non verbal, and non physical, facets of communication that encourage obedience to any suggested course of action, the first and most important is the listeners subconscious, or inner, "TRUST" in the person who is offering them the suggestion. The person being suggested too is responding almost entirely emotionally to the personal magnetism of the person making the suggestion to them.

Secondly, is the listener's emotional acceptance on a subconscious level, of the person making the suggestion as being an authority, or a leader. The recipient of any suggestion must, at least sub consciously, emotionally accept the suggesting person as someone who has, in some undefined way, a kind of right of direction, or an authority of command, over him or her.

Briefly, many people will quickly accept suggestions when commands given to them would be either resented or ignored. Suggestions are almost always accepted when given by those people who display what we may call "personal magnetism," even when these same suggestions would be either rejected, or ignored, if they came from a person who did not display this very useful personality trait.

This personal magnetism, charisma, charm, presence, or whatever else you may wish to call it, may be understood to be a characteristic that has a great, if not a dominant, importance to those who have conceived within themselves a desire to lead others. Those who would be leaders must develop as much of their personal magnetism as they possibly can if they wish to attain the goals of leadership that they believe they desire to reach.

Inherent Personal Magnetism

Personal magnetism is something that some people seem to just have, while many other people do not seem to have any magnetism at all. It is actually a feeling of personal trust, a non-physical thing, that other people may sense, or feel, instinctively. It can usually be noted immediately on meeting a person who possesses this highly beneficial personal characteristic. Personal magnetism seems to radiate around the one who possesses it, creating the sub conscious confidence of other people in them. Personal magnetism may also be called the real power of personality, in that it is always present in those who are the real leaders of the world. In addition, this magnetism seems to always be absent in those whose destiny is to only follow others.

Physical Appearance

Personal magnetism does not ever depend upon personal appearance. However, personal magnetism is always enhanced by a good personal appearance. People judge others by their appearance. The person who wishes to lead must look like a leader to those he wishes to follow him.

An attractive and impressive physical appearance, coupled with imposing and attractive dress, a commanding attitude, and a fine speaking voice, are all very important personal assets. These may truly provide a favorable contribution to a person's attraction, and an enhancement of their natural personal magnetism. Still, these fine outward physical attributes may only be superficial indications of the true power of the individuals' real personality. These physical indications must be backed up by that indefinable something, those non-physical properties, as we may refer to them, which separate those people who possess real personal magnetism from those who do not.

People may go out of their way to "Dress for Success," master public speaking, and condition their bodies to a fine physical edge, and still not develop the kind of personal magnetism that gives them the immediate trust and confidence of those whom they contact in their daily life. Until the non-physical and insensible properties of the person are also honed, they will still be unable to gain and maintain the immediate trust and respect of others.

People With Magnetic Personalities

If you recall from history some of the qualities of the most magnetic leaders of business and government over the past half century; national leaders like Roosevelt, Kennedy, and Churchill, to name but a few, you can understand what natural personal magnetism really is. No political figure ever really succeeds without having it. Personal magnetism is one of the fundamental attributes that lead to real success in the world. It draws other people to the one who has it. As one of the fundamental attributes of success in human affairs that has been given to mankind, it is also something that may be learned and mastered in a lifetime. It is not a trait that is to be possessed only by those whom their creator has blessed with it at birth.

You probably can recognize at first sight, or at first meeting, those who have personal magnetism. In your mind, you will find that you are separating these people immediately from those who do not possess this magnetism. Most people who have personal magnetism display it at first sight. Their magnetism surrounds them like an armor of power that they carry with them into every situation. You should make it your business to begin to develop your own personal magnetism, by observing these people with magnetic personalities, and judging just what qualities of personal magnetism they have. One of the most interesting things that I have discovered is that those who are born with a decent quantity of personal magnetism usually do not attempt to develop it further. They seem to be satisfied with whatever they have been given by their creator.

This is undoubtedly unfortunate, as it is entirely possible for anyone to develop or increase whatever quantity of personal magnetism that they have been born with. In this way, these people, or anyone else, may expand their personal magnetism so that more and more people naturally see them as being trustworthy, or worthy of respect. Developing the personal magnetism that you have been born with is certainly one way of mastering yourself and learning to develop yourself in life.

Developing Your Own Personal Magnetism

All living human beings have at least a modicum of personal magnetism within themselves. Those who desire to grow and prosper themselves in the world can cultivate this modicum, regardless of how large or small it may be. By carefully tending their natural personal magnetism, they can allow it to gain its full growth. Then, gradually, and with great care, they can bring their personal magnetism to fruition, and display it to the world, to gain the world's trust and respect.

Personal magnetism is a trait that is more valuable than personal wealth, as it is something that once developed can never be taken away. It is also something that may never be either regulated or taxed. Personal magnetism is certainly a trait that is well worth the time and effort that is spent in its cultivation. Personal Magnetism is something that will always become the primary stepping-stone of future growth and opportunity in the life of the person who possesses it.

Like all personal traits that are really worth cultivating, personal magnetism will not grow spontaneously in anyone. It must always be nurtured and developed within the person who wishes to cultivate their natural personal magnetism. However, this is something which is only accomplished thorough the long process of slow and faithful effort. The person who wishes to develop this most useful trait is always moving toward the goal of possessing and using more and more personal magnetism in their daily life. Like any other valuable trait, personal magnetism must be consciously cultivated in the fertile soil of the fundamental character of the person who wishes to attain the goal of permanently possessing it.

The Prime Attribute:—Self Confidence

Personal magnetism will grow only in those who are self confident, those who are certain that possessing personal magnetism is something that is theirs by right. Those who wish to cultivate personal magnetism must first cultivate self-confidence, by firmly believing in themselves, and in their own abilities.

To accept that you have real abilities is not egoism. It is but realizing something that is a fact. To believe that you actually have abilities that are in fact imaginary is egoism. Every egoism that you possess is something that is always destructive to your real self. By following the well-known adage: "To thine own self be true," you will find that you can accept your own real skills and abilities, without boasting of them to others, and without puffing them up beyond what they actually are.

Self-confidence, decisiveness, action, and a strong mind, will always attract people to you. Indecisiveness, and inactivity, will always turn people away from you. You must cultivate self-confidence by first firmly resolving to accomplish whatever task you concentrate your mind upon. Do not ever even think of the possibility of failure. Instead, resolve to bring to a successful conclusion whatever task you may begin. You must master the art of being habitually successfully in all your endeavors. You may accomplish this by successfully completing even the most trivial of the tasks you may undertake in your daily life, whatever they may be.

Building The Habit of Success

Reaching success in any accomplishment always adds to the strength of your character. Failure to complete a task, failing to complete even the smallest task, diminishes everything that you have ever accomplished. The person who would have a magnetic personality must think only of gaining ultimate success in everything that they attempt. You must always remember how directly your thoughts shape your actions. Think only of your success. Ignore the slightest possibility of your failing in anything that you may attempt. You must know that you can, and that you will, solve any problem that ever presents itself to you.

Personal Magnetism can only become an active power in the lives of those who are self confident, decisive, active, and strong-minded. Those who are weak willed, indecisive and uncertain about things in their life will never be able to develop even the slight natural amount of personal magnetism they may have been granted at birth. The plant of personal magnetism cannot flourish in the poor soil of a weak, failing, and indecisive personality.

Mental Clarity

If you desire to develop personal magnetism, you must master clear thinking. This requires that you bring to an end any internal conversations and mental debates you may have within yourself. You must end all of these internal mental debates, regardless of what they may concern. Your mind at present may well be clouded and confused, wavering, and debating internally on any and every subject. To end this random debate you must form firm opinions on any subject that you may have heretofore been indecisive about. These firm opinions must be opinions that you will now firmly hold, until the overwhelming evidence of experience forces you to exchange one of these firmly held opinions for another that you will then hold to just as firmly.

You must develop within yourself a decisive and positive character. You must learn to make all of your decisions cleanly, without any indecision, quibble, or hesitation. You must realize that making an incorrect decision is always better, and more worthwhile, than hesitating, procrastinating, and eventually making no decision at all. To demonstrate a strong and forceful magnetic character, you must become a fount of decisive speech, and real, meaningful, strong willed actions.

You must learn to always:

Decide without delay, and execute without misgivings.

This one step alone will give you an advantage in all of your affairs, raising you over the majority of people. If you observe people closely, you will soon discover that most people find it difficult to firmly decide on anything at all. So long as you are of this class, you will have no chance of success. Being firm and decisive makes it possible for you to move forward confidently in life.

Even the most limited degree of natural personal magnetism can be developed by anyone, regardless of the station in life in which they find themselves. Magnetism of character is not dependent upon either the physical appearance, or the formal education of the one who decides to develop it. Personal magnetism, as history proves, can be very strongly developed in those who have both a poor appearance, and a lack of formal education.

Personal magnetism is a personality trait that is dependent upon neither education nor appearance, but it is a trait that may usually be enhanced by either improving your physical appearance or gaining a formal education. You must not either despise or mourn the supposed advantages of an attractive appearance, or of a well-educated mind, as they may apply in your own case. These attributes, valuable as they may be, have nothing to do with your becoming magnetic, and attracting to you the admiration and best wishes of all whom meet you.

Auto Suggestion and Self Hypnosis

Autosuggestion, using affirmations, and self hypnosis may be of some assistance in developing personal magnetism, but objective introspection is a considerably better course of action to follow if you sincerely wish to bring personal magnetism firmly into your life. Turning your eye inward, and discovering those places in your character where you find that you are weak, so that you can work diligently to strengthen them, will be of considerably more benefit to your development than simply repeating parrot phrases concerning the desired improvements you wish to make in your life. Self-improvement must become an overwhelming desire in your life. It may not ever be a casual goal. It is never a goal that you hope you will reach someday, without extending any real effort toward reaching it.

The game of life is a game that is played for keeps. It is a continuous game, not one that allows rest breaks or refreshment stops during which you may let down your guard, or stop your efforts toward gaining real success in life. The person who seriously wishes to develop personal magnetism must take the game of life very seriously indeed. They must be willing to devote both the time and effort required to really developing themselves. They must do this always, with an eye on their goals in the future. The success bound person realizes that working for self-development or not, the sands of time will pass them by in any event. They know that they will not have made any gains in their real character over time, unless they have worked hard for those gains that they may attain by their own efforts. No one may assist you in your personal growth. You must realize that your ultimate success in life is always entirely in your hands.

Your Voice

You must develop your voice, so that you may use it for its intended purpose, to communicate with others. Have you ever taken the time to listen to yourself speak? You should do so, as you may find the experience to be quite interesting. Learning to speak properly and decisively is as important to your personal magnetism as is learning to make a decision. You may find it worthwhile to use a tape recorder to hear yourself speak under various conditions of your life. Listen to your voice to rid yourself of any defects of articulation, intonation, and accent, which you may have acquired. Observe how you speak to different people under different conditions of your life.

No other human possession equals the voice in its ability to influence others. If you would lead others, you must deliberately cultivate leadership in your voice. A well modulated, firm, and decisive voice, with a pleasing and sociable personal manner, will always attract those whom you wish to influence to follow your desires.

Self Control

Personally, magnetic people always possess a high degree of self-control. These people never indulge in random outbursts of passion. The truly magnetic personality is always in control of their outwardly calm emotional nature. When aroused by others, instead of displaying anger, they will usually lapse into silence. Occasionally answering those who rally against them, these people are more frequently silent except for a few well-chosen words, words most frequently spoken in a soft and gentle voice. To truly develop personal magnetism you must always develop your self-control.

The person with great personal magnetism always displays all of the positive characteristics of a well-developed, well-balanced, human being. They may always be thoughtful of themselves, but they are always conscious and considerate of others. They are calm, self confident, self-approving, and sufficient unto themselves. These qualities of character show forth in the truly magnetic person, and other people sense them immediately. They are the qualities of character that are apparent to everyone, and do not ever need to be explained.

Anger and Strong Emotions

Anger is far from the heart of the truly magnetic person. They realize that anger is the most limiting of human emotions, and they usually do not consider it to be worth expressing to others. The truly magnetic person displays anger only as the conscious rational choice of an emotion to display, to gain a particular desired effect. They always display anger to others only to gain some purpose of their own. Anger is never something that overtakes them and dominates them through the force of their emotions. Internal anger, or the desire to control others, never carries them away. They may use anger purposely, as to gain a point, or to encourage an action, but they do not feel the destructive inner emotion of any form of anger that they may consciously display.

As anger is always the result of discovering that another person is opposing your desires for them. Once you truly understand that you can never really control another person, you realize that anger really has no use in your life. Understanding how little control that a person actually has over their life, much less over the life of another, is of the utmost importance to real personal growth. Only when the lack of real control in life is understood, and the desire to become angry or to feel outrage is recognized for what it is, an egoism, can a person release this desire and become really successful in their life.

Focus of Attention

The truly magnetic person has the ability to focus their attention completely on the person they are speaking to. This allows them to gain, without any real effort, the full trust and confidence of other people. By directing the full focus of their attention to those to whom they speak, the recipient of their attention is more open to, and considerably more susceptible to, any suggestions that the magnetic person may wish to give them.

Most people do not focus their attention on others when they speak, nor do they listen to others when other people are speaking. By focusing your attention on the one whom you are speaking to, and by listening intently to them when they speak, you are both learning about the person, and paying attention to them. You are giving them attention in a way that they have rarely have ever had attention paid to them in the past. The response of people to this attention, directed exclusively to them, is usually exceptionally positive.

Observing Others

To cultivate your own personal magnetism, you must study those who attract you, those people who you believe are personally magnetic. You must observe these people to discover what elements in their characters attract you to them. You must then work to make the beneficial elements you observe in them a part of your own character. You should never simply imitate the other person's actions, but you should emulate the positive examples they present to you, doing so in your own way.

Lessons just as valuable to your development should also be drawn from those who repel you. There is always a reason for feeling repulsion toward another person, whether it is either physical repulsion or social repulsion. You will do well to begin by deliberately avoiding imitating any of those traits that you find to be repulsive in others. If someone repulses you in any way, it is quite probable that they also repulse many other people.

Once you firmly decide to develop a magnetic personality, you are already on the way to doing so. By your very decision to develop yourself, you have taken the first step. Your ability to make a firm decision, and stick to it, will help to carry you the rest of the way. Now you must just stay on this course, following the suggestions given above, and you will find that within a few years you will have developed your own personal magnetism to a greater degree than you might originally have thought possible. By firmly willing the development of a magnetic personality, and by accomplishing the detailed work that its development requires you will eventually manifest your own magnetic personality to the world.

CHAPTER THREE

Fascination And Charming

According to Cornelius Agrippa, as he states in his first book of occult Philosophy:

> "Fascination is a binding which comes from the spirit of the witch, through the eyes of him that is so bewitched, and entering to his heart."
> Occult Philosophy or Magic
> Samuel Weiser, Inc.
> New York, NY 1971

From his description, fascination seems to be a sort of Cupid's arrow, one of either love or lust. In my opinion, fascination and charming as occult techniques are actually quite a bit more than that. I do not believe that their use must be limited only to occasions of love and lust.

Fascination and charming are a particular set of useful magical techniques. They are both useful in projecting specific thoughts, sending general 'vibrations or feelings,' transmitting mental 'psychic energies,' or even issuing mental commands into the minds of other people. These are obviously very worthwhile abilities to have, and they are certainly worth the brief time they take to develop.

These techniques seem to work best with others when you are in the physical presence of the subject. This seems to be because you are obtaining instant feedback from them concerning the effect of your efforts. However, they may also be used successfully when you are not physically near the subject.

The techniques of fascination and charming make use of those basic lessons that you pass through on the road to developing yourself as a magician. While the ultimate application of most of these exercises is directed to other magical techniques, in the techniques of fascination and charming, these exercises are applied directly to the direction and projection of our own thoughts and desires into the minds and consciousness of others.

Almost everyone wants to be thought a fascinating and charming person. Using these mental techniques is certainly the fastest way for a magician to gain this end.

Fascination Through the Projected Thought

From in your mind the strongly willed thought:

> You find me to be a charming and interesting person.
> You desire to get to know me better.

Energize this thought as an energized thought form, by placing as much emotional energy into it as you can. Then carry this thought around with you, wearing it on your forehead as if it were a billboard. When you see someone to whom you wish to apply this thoughtform, move the thought slowly from your forehead over the top of your head to the nape of your neck. Then release the thought form to that person, along with the willed direction that it go to them and that they accept it. You release this thoughtform as mentioned before, by passing the thoughtform over the top of your head to the nape of your neck, and then releasing it with directions as to whom it is to go, and that the recipient accept the thoughtform. With a little practice, you will find that this is a simple and effective method of sending thoughts to another person.

The short two-line thought given above is about the longest thoughtform that can be vitalized and carried around with you all day. Should you be able to create and use a shorter general thoughtform to good advantage in your daily life, you should make one up and use it. A long thoughtform does not have the same sharp and intense effect that a sort thoughtform has. A short and simple thought form will always work best.

You must be aware that over half the people you transmit your thought form to will not receive it correctly, as their minds are too full of other things, or for other people, their subconscious will not notify their conscious mind of the receipt of the thoughtform. Those people whose mind is full of sub conscious and conscious chatter will not be able to receive the thoughtform clearly either. Unfortunately, this includes the great bulk of humanity.

What happens is that the thoughtform is received, and filed away, without being noticed by the conscious mind. Inside the person's mind, they usually accept the thoughtform as one of their own random thoughts. If there is no great objection to that thoughtform as a thought of the person, they will accept it as an observation, and then often bring it to the conscious attention of the individual as a part of the continual random chatter occurring in the mind. In this way, the person cannot distinguish between the thoughtform that has been sent them and their own random thoughts.

You have identified the thought as a foreign thought when you say:

> You find me to be a charming and interesting person.
> You desire to get to know me better.

However, if they do not disagree with or oppose that thought, the person receiving the thought will usually change it around, adopting the thought as their own. Thus, the received thought becomes:

> I find you a charming and interesting person.
> I desire to get to know you better.

Should that be the thought that you send to the person, they will accept it as something complimentary to themselves, and file it away in that manner. In this case, they will not apply it to you, believing only that you like and wish to know them. This is unlikely to be what you wish to occur.

The simpler and shorter the thought the better, but accurately selecting the thought that you wish to use in your daily life is even more important. You should put some time into deciding exactly what thoughtform you want to use before you begin using one. You must remember that you are going to be carrying that thoughtform around with you, 'as if it were a billboard,' and to some extent, it will influence everyone whom you meet. Your thoughtform will influence others, at least slightly, whether or not you directly send it to them. As a vitalized thought form, it will strengthen any other thoughts of the same or similar nature that anyone may have about you. This is actually the result you are looking for. You must be aware that this means that you do not always have to send the thoughtform out to someone to have it result in at least some slight effect on him or her. If you think of the thoughtform as a billboard you are wearing, you can get the idea of how it will work on most people. They will notice it, whether or not they pay any attention to it.

To keep the thoughtform working at peak efficiency, you should remember to revitalize the thoughtform during the day. Adding emotional energy to it will keep it active and working for you. The best practice is to leave the house with the thoughtform vitalized, then revitalize it just before lunch, and again before leaving work at the end of the day, if you desire to have the thoughtform carry into the evening.

Some brief useful thought forms of this type are:

> You find me charming.
> You want to know me better.
> You respect my abilities.
> You like me.
> You know that I am competent.
> You trust my judgment.
> You like my work.

These and other similar short and to the point thoughtforms are good general-purpose thoughtforms for anyone to use on a daily basis, especially in a working enviroment.

Once you have attracted the attention of the person you wish to attract, it is easy to form other thoughtforms to send them while you are conversing with them. While listening intently to the other person, focusing your attention on them, you can be forming other thoughtforms to send them. Once the person has a developed the desired interest in you, you can cool off any possibly unwanted romantic ardor by sending them thoughts concerning your competency and your ability to work. Women can also cool off male ardor by sending the man thoughts indicating that he respects her.

> You know how competent I am.
> You recognize that I am a good worker.
> You find that you really respect me.
> You respect me for my skill and ability.

Most men seem not to wish to become romantically involved with women whom they believe that they respect. I personally do not think that this says a lot about where the state of man / woman relationships are in our society, but that seems to be the way that it is. Thus, it seems that these respect thoughtforms can shift a relationship away from following any possible romantic tack. Thoughtforms that make other people think of you as a worker or as a drone that they can use, may also get you out of situations where spite, jealousy or envy may be present. One of my female students successfully directed the following thoughtform to a woman who was not happy with the way she was leading a meeting:

> You know she is not pretty, but she is competent.

The process of fascination through focusing thoughtforms to others can be very rewarding, and it can certainly make your path in life considerably easier.

Projection Of A Particular Vibration Or Energy

If you think about it, there are several fundamental vibrations which you already have surrounding you. For example, there is the vibration of mental energy, concentrated around your head. The sexual vibration around your genitals is another. Your wallet, whether full or empty, has a money vibration to it. You may have other vibrations connected to you, if you think about it. You would just have to take the time to think what they might be. If you wish to send one of these vibrations, into the room or directly to another person, you can easily do so.

Visualize the particular vibration you wish to send to another person. As an example, if it be the mental vibration, to convince them of your intelligence or brainpower, visualize your mind, and transmit the visualization to the other person by breathing. Do this as if you were sending them the specific energy of your mind. Energizing the thought with breathing, to gain more energy for the thought, does this quite well. If you project the thoughtform that they should accept the specific energy, along with the energy itself, they will usually take the projected energy into themselves without difficulty. Thoughtforms that you might project to another person, along with the energy of a specific vibration are:

You will like this.
This is interesting.
You agree with this.
We agree on this.

These projections may be used to convince or sway people in argument, as well as to have them turn their minds in the specific direction that you desire.

Projection of the Chakra Energy

Another form of energy projection that is very effective is projection of the chakra energy. In this case, it is probably best not to visualize the energy leaving a specific chakra. Instead, I visualize the projection of the kind of energy that corresponds to a particular chakra. One day I had a sore throat, and I was speaking to someone. I was aware that my voice was not particularly pleasant. During a lull in the conversation, I projected to them the thought that they enjoyed my throat energy, and were soothed by it. Later in the conversation, the person mentioned that they thought that I had a soothing voice. I thought that it sounded like sand paper myself, which was why I had projected the thought about my throat energy to them.

On another occasion, I had to speak with and comfort someone who was in a state of great emotional distress. I began by projecting heart energy and a thought of emotional compassion to them as I approached them. During our conversation, I was able to take their hand, and I reinforced my compassionate feeling for their current emotional difficulty through light physical contact as well. The person responded well to my words. Later on, they thanked me for my assistance and emotional support at what had been a trying time for them.

This technique is useful in your daily life, as it will make your path through life quite a bit easier. These same techniques are useful in preparing people to listen to what you have to say to them. A heavy preliminary dose of mental energy makes other people want to hear what you are going to say.

Commanding Through Projection Of Thoughtforms

An energized thought form can be sent to another person as a command. The more energized the thoughtform is, the more immediately and directly the command will affect the person. However, it is best if the thoughtform is also accompanied by a verbal command. Otherwise, the person may find himself or herself reacting, or trying to react, to words that they have not heard. This is sufficiently disconcerting to the average person that they may not react to the command at all.

This technique may be used in an emergency, with or without a verbal command. In this case, the person will probably attribute the thoughtform to an angel, a saint, or some other spiritual agency. In any case, once they sense the emergency, their emotions are usually sufficiently stimulated so that they are unlikely to look for the source of the thought.

I use this technique whenever I see a potentially dangerous situation, such as a person in danger of being hit by an automobile, or even a person who is walking so near the curb they are about to get splattered with water. Most people will react without thought to an energized thoughtform command. In an emergency, people only very rarely, if ever, recognize that the thought that motivated them was not there own. A friend of mine said he once had the experience of being thanked for a warning thoughtform he had sent to a person. This was the only time I have ever heard of it happening. I can say that it has never happened to me.

Suggestions

Energized thoughtforms, used as suggestions, rather than as commands, are much easier for people to deal with in their daily life. These thoughtform suggestions, like the series of suggestions given below, can be used, even one after another, to "soften up" another person for your later approach to them.

> I like the name Frank.
> Men named Frank have good taste.
> A Man named Frank can help me in my work.
> Frank knows advertising, and can help me with
>   my advertising campaign.
> Frank knows how to get me the greatest returns
>   for my advertising dollar.
> I want Frank to handle my advertising.

A student sent this series of thoughtforms successively to the same person. He began sending them to him as he left his office to go to the office of a potential client for a presentation on their account. The last thoughtform was sent to the person as they all sat down at the conference table for the presentation meeting. My student received the account from the firm.

Less complex suggestions can also be used, as can less forceful commands. The difference between them is simply in how you word the suggestion, or phrase the command. A few actual examples used by my students follow.

In a social situation where a friend protests that she is cold and wants to leave a party, while my student wants to stay:

> You are getting warmer.
> You are quite warm.
> You are warm and comfortable.
> You are enjoying yourself.

The student stayed, and his friend enjoyed the party.

In another situation, where my student really wanted to go home from a boring party, but her date wanted to stay:

> You are getting very tired.
> You have to be up early tomorrow.
> You can hardly keep your eyes open.
> You had better go to sleep soon.
> You really want to go home.

My student and her date left the party soon afterwards, as soon as the last though had fully penetrated his mind. Her date even napped in the cab on the way home.

CHAPTER FOUR

Partial Astral Projection

The technique of partial projection of the astral body, that is a prelude to actually learning astral projection, can be used alone, or it may be combined with the projection of a vibe or a thoughtform, to obtain interesting and amusing effects. This combination of techniques is best developed if it is first practiced with an intimate friend, who is also a magician, until it is mastered. The combination has it's greatest, and most dramatic, effect when it is used in situations where the person who is receiving all of the magician's attention has no idea at all of what is actually happening to them.

This requires that the person using the technique must be skilled in their practice of the technique before they attempt to apply it to anyone. The problem with this technique is that you can become so involved in watching the results you are getting from using the technique that you can break off doing it in mid stride. In this respect, I would suppose that it is a good technique to use to further develop your metal focus.

At the agency where two of my students were formerly employed, they had a boss who was very straight laced, and whose attitude toward women was less enlightened than his attitude toward the office furniture. His secretary of many years was a woman of the same small-minded type. Another magician, who was both a co-worker, a fellow student, and a good friend, joined my student and decided that they would practice this technique together until they mastered it thoroughly, simply for the purpose of applying it to these two Victorian minded slave drivers. It took several months of hard work for them to fully master the technique, but they finally managed to do it.

A few weeks after they had mastered the thought and partial projection technique, their rigid and narrow-minded boss called them into one of the firms regular monthly meetings. He had his secretary taking notes of the meeting, as usual. As soon as the meeting was underway, the two students began partial astral projection along with simultaneous vibe projection on both the boss and his secretary. They both projected their hands to various parts of the two victims anatomy, while sending them as heavy a sexual vibrations as they could muster. The meeting was a total flop, as the boss became visibly aroused, and quickly had difficulty even speaking. The secretary began trembling in her chair shortly after the meeting started, and left the room within a few moments, excusing herself to her lord and master by telling him that she had been suddenly taken ill.

Several of the people who were at the meeting commented later on the bosses actions at the meeting. My students said only that he must have been having an off day and publicly left it at that. Obviously, they did not want anyone to know what they had been up to. At a victory dinner that evening, my students went into gales of laughter over their successful prank.

This technique has great potential for fun and games, but it has very little practical application that I have ever heard of. One of my male students told me that he often uses the technique of partial projection at restaurants and singles bars. He told me on several occasions that he enjoys having fun with it.

I have not used this technique often, but like the other techniques in my ever-expanding magical tool kit, it is available for me whenever I find that I might need to use it. One of the positive uses for this technique is reaching out to touch or sense something that may be out of reach or even dangerous to handle. This involves projecting your hand out to carefully touch whatever you wish. There is a certain amount of sensory feed back in this technique, but it is certainly not nearly as strong as would be found if you were physically touching the object.

I believe that practicing this touch technique on surfaces of different textures might allow this sense of touch to be developed further. Using hard wood, stone, cotton wool and fabrics might be of use to gain this end. As with all else, practice here would probe or disprove my theory that this could be a useful non physical sense of touch.

On the other hand, mastering this technique for the occasional handling of remote objects apparently has little inducement, compared to mastering the technique so that you can have fun in bars, at parties, and other places.

CHAPTER FIVE

The Magic Of Stones

Stones were said by the ancients to be the bones of our mother, the good earth, whose breast nourishes us and gives us our food. Those who live close to the land may recognize the blessing of mans dominion over the earth as the caretaker of the divine creation more easily. It is even more especially understood by those 'plain folk,' who live their lives in harmony with their creator. These people live their lives on their farms as our ancestors did, at least to as great an extent as they may do so in our modern technological world.

One of these plain people visited me one day, and we spoke of the way that he practiced magic using stones. As he spoke, with his permission, I took a number of notes, and it is from this conversation that the following information is given. He told me that he had seven bowls in his home, each containing a specific stone of power. In addition, he had his white 'name stone' hidden underneath the table containing the other seven stones. The man was quite interesting, and to my mind, a very religious person. The information he so freely gave to me is given below.

It is the premise of the animist philosophy that everything has a divine soul, and a God given spiritual nature within it. This philosophy applies to the entire created universe, including many things that are not believed to be living by most people. Things such as stones, as well as trees, and plants, are all credited with having a spiritual nature. Because these things do not move of their own power, or are not able to communicate with cries or words to others, many people believe that they are not alive. In fact, they are actually all very much alive. Each kind of being within the creation lives within its own natural kingdom, either the animal kingdom, which includes man, the vegetable kingdom, which includes all living plants, or the mineral kingdom, which includes all earth and stones.

God the creator created all of these things, as well as creating the entire visible and invisible universe. This animist concept of spiritual life permeating the life of all three of nature's kingdoms naturally follows from this. This idea expresses that in the universe there is only God, who ultimately created all that there is. It then follows that as God made everything from his own substance, the entire universe is a part of the creator, both materially and spiritually. This animist conception of the universe is therefore fully compatible with all orthodox Christian doctrine.

It also follows that all things that the creator has made have been placed there to be useful in some manner for man. For it is man whom God has set over the whole of the earthly creation, by his creator. Having been given the responsibility of tending the divine creation, it is man's task to use all of these many living things that permeate the whole creation to the benefit of himself, as well as to the benefit of the rest of the divine creation. Yet man must realize that in doing so, he is always working to the greater glory of the Lord God, his creator.

The authority of human kind over the physically manifested divine creation is mentioned in the Bible. This authority is shown in the eighth Psalm, verses three to eight. The specific verse of dominion, (which it is useful for a person to know), is the sixth verse of the eighth Psalm. It is my understanding that in Islam, the religion taught by the Prophet Mohammed, there is a similar verse in their holy book, the Koran. This shows that the dominion of God is recognizably granted to all of his creation. For as our Lord God has apportioned both the beliefs of religions, and the various forms of worship out to mankind, the fact of human domination over the creation was also revealed equally to all of mankind in their holy books. It is not widely known or well accepted by most people that this domination of mankind, granted them over the whole of the divine creation, extends out to the finest things of the creation. Domination extends even unto the grains of sand of the ocean. It extends as well to each of the pebbles and stones to be found in the earth.

Now the importance of supposedly inanimate stones in our world may be shown by the large number of times that stones are cited in holy scripture, both simply as stones, and also by name, as to the kind of stone that is meant. My own concordance, not an expensive one, lists sixty five citations for the word stone, showing that they are indeed important in the scheme of the divine creation. The concordance has citations for the word stone in books from Genesis to Revelation. Many of these Bible citations also reveal to the knowing eye the manner in which various stones are to be used by mankind to his benefit.

Genesis 28:11 through verse 22 tell the story of Jacob's sleeping at the place he later called Bethel (Beth El). Using a stone as his pillow, Jacob had a dream of a ladder to heaven that came upon him as he slept there. On awakening, Jacob set up the stone he had used as his pillow, and anointed it by pouring oil on it. (Verse 18) Then, naming the place Bethel, he made an agreement with the lord of that place, the spirit possessor of that stone, that it should be his God. He promised to tithe to the spirit of the stone, giving it a tenth of his increase. In the scripture, it is said that Jacob knew that the spirit of God was in that place.

The very stone, which was once Jacob's pillow, is now said to be the coronation stone of the monarchs of England. They have brought it from Scotland, and located it under their throne chair, where it is known as the Stone of Scone. As the stone served Jacob, so it now serves the British state. However, it seems that the British no longer tithe to that stone. It may well be believed that if they did, they would have increase and prosperity, instead of the shame and dishonor that has recently come on the royal house of that nation.

Genesis 31:44-55 tells about Jacob raising another pillar. This stone was to serve as a witness to the covenant that was made between Jacob and Laban, whose daughter Rachel, Jacob had taken for his wife. In this case, the stone was raised for a witness pillar, and with a heap of stones placed around it, it was to serve as a witness of the oath that Jacob and Laban swore to each other on that solemn occasion.

Thus we can see that a stone may contain the mighty spirit of the deity of a place, as it did at Beth El, or it may serve as a witness to an oath, as it did at Galeed; witnessing the covenant between Jacob and Laban. In another place, Joshua 24:25-27 a stone is once again set up as a witness to a covenant, or an agreement, made between people. The use of stones as witnesses to a covenant or an agreement is seen through these several examples to have been quite common in Bible times.

In Genesis 49:24, Joseph is praised as an archer, and is further said to be a shepherd and the stone of Israel. In being called the stone of Israel, Joseph is said to be the one person upon whom the nation of Israel was to be founded. Referring to someone as a stone, when the meaning was that they were the foundation of an enterprise, or even as in this case of a nation, was considered a great compliment to them. We recall that Jesus Christ called Simon Peter the rock upon which he would found his church. Thus, as Joseph became the foundation of Israel, so did Simon Peter become the foundation of Christianity.

The building of Solomon's house is described in I Kings 7. It is mentioned that it had many costly stones for its foundation. In Israel, where few trees grew to any size, and where wood has always been at a premium, large stones were used for the foundations of buildings. The building of the Temple to the Lord God is described in I Chronicles 22: 1-19. The first task undertaken was the hewing or quarrying of stones, as is mentioned in verse two.

In Numbers (15:35 and 35:17), casting stones on a person is mentioned as a punishment among the Israelites. Stoning a criminal became the commonly accepted method of putting to death someone who was convicted of a crime. In the course of time, it passed from being a punishment continued to the victim's death, as it was for St. Steven, the first martyr to Christianity, to being used occasionally just to drive someone out of town, as it was when St. Paul was stoned.

I Samuel 17:40, tells the story of David choosing five stones from a brook. One of these stones became the very stone with which he later killed the Giant Goliath. This is one reason why brook and river stones are thought to be more powerful than ordinary stones. Stones projected from slings have been used as weapons since very ancient times. For this kind of work, smooth river stones are favored even to this day.

At Psalm 118:22 is mentioned the old middle eastern story of the stone that the builders rejected, which later became the headstone of the course, the cornerstone, or the keystone, depending on the particular rendition of the story you happen to hear. The retelling of this tale, now referring to Christ as the headstone of all creation, and implying his rejection as the Messiah by the Jews, is to be found in all of the synoptic Gospels. It is located at Matthew 21:42, Mark 12:10, Luke 20:17. It is also told once again in Peter 2:7.

I think that all of this repetition symbolizing Christ as the headstone is to make certain that the reader gets the point. However, most Bible scholars today believe that these repetitions of this ancient tale are all textual interpolations. They believe that they were added into the synoptic Gospels in the time of the great textual change of the bible, which happened between about 180 AD and 380 AD. At this time, the bible was severely edited and extensively revised. It is this revised version that we have today.

This is a general sampling of the appearance of stones in the Bible. You can find more of these references with a concordance, and I have run across several references to stones that were not found in my concordance, by just reading casually through the Bible. Now I will deal with the references to stones that have to do with what is called magic. I must say first that what is called magic is actually just using the things of the earth, such as stones, properly, and always according to their God given power.

In Revelations 2:17, it is mentioned that to those who overcome the temptations of the earth shall be given a white stone, with a new name written inside of it, and no man shall know this name except the one who receives it. From this is taken the idea that people who would use stones to do magical work with must first find themselves a white stone, preferably a brook stone. The stone must be one that has sufficient surface that they may write their given name on the outside of it, usually with a black pen. This means that the stone should be at least about an inch and a half in diameter. Then they are to take this stone and wash it, removing all dirt, and dry it carefully. Then they should write their given name on the stone. That same night that they find the stone, they should sleep with it in their bed, so that they may get a dream of another name. The spirit of the stone gives the dream, and their new name to them. It is this name which is to be found within the white stone.

Now many people who know of this work, and who follow it, teach that once the name is given, the white stone is then to be placed in a leather bag. It is to be placed together with the person's most sacred possessions, and quite naturally hidden away out of sight. The person should not show this white stone to anyone, for fear that the person they show it to may touch the stone, or harm it through their envy or jealousy.

After receiving their new name, the person who gets the new name never thinks of himself by his old name again. From that time forward he is to think of himself always by his new name. He will continue to use his old name in his daily life however, and he will still speak of himself as having his old name, to all whom he knows. In that way, the new name, as given him by the spirit of the stone in a dream, is both his new name and is a secret name, one that is known to him alone.

Now this is the way of the one who would work with stones who is a Christian, and who therefore knows that Jesus Christ is the cornerstone of the world. This person believes and accepts that Christ is the cornerstone of every house, of every congregation, and of every temple. Through this, it may be understood that

Jesus Christ is the very cornerstone of this whole earth. Therefore, Christ being the cornerstone, every rock, pebble and grain of sand is like a brother to Jesus Christ in this work. It is only necessary to ask any stone what it is made to do for you, and it will answer truly to you, telling you what power has been granted it for the benefit of humankind by God the creator.

When the time comes to ask the stone to do work, it always depends firstly on what is within the province of the stone to accomplish. For that which the stone may do, it will accomplish speedily for the one who has brought it forth, and to whom it has given a name. But if it not be within the province of the stone to accomplish that which is required, then the man who has the white stone must ask his stone to seek out another stone, one that has the power required for the work which is to be accomplished. Then the man may also bring that stone forth, finding it wherever he is led to it. In this way, he will make the new stone his aid in that particular matter that he has in mind to accomplish. In doing this work, the stone accomplishes that which the Lord God has set for it to do in the interest, and to the benefit, of all mankind.

For just as a man gains merit with his Lord by being of assistance to other men, so does the spirit of a stone gain merit and grace by helping mankind attain whatever it desires. Therefore, this is not evil magic, but indeed, it is a practice that the Lord God has ordained to be beneficial to the entire world. With stones, all is accomplished under the grace of God, and with the blessings of Jesus Christ. Therefore, do not ever hesitate to ask your white stone for assistance should you ever need help from it at any time at all. It will be both pleased and delighted to assist you in attaining whatever the Lord God has opened out to you.

Now if a stone is to be a witness, it is first to be anointed with oil, (Gen. 31:44-55) and then the pledge or covenant is to be made before it. When a stone is acting as a witness, it shall truly cry out of the wall, (Habk. 2:11) if the pledge or covenant to which it is a witness is either voided or transgressed. The procedure for this work is old, and is well established in the Bible.

Many instances of raising a stone as a pillar to witness a covenant are cited in the Bible, beginning with the pillar of Jacob and Laban, which I have mentioned previously. An oath or contract, a pledge or covenant, that is made in this way is witnessed by the stone, and thus is enforced by the earth itself. No man should ever even consider breaking such a solemn pledge, for the whole earth would rise up against him as an oath breaker.

I have since learned other things about working with stones that my plain folk friend did not tell me of. I mention them here, to complete this information. Other stones used in this work, especially those used for healing, require a restoration of their energies, or their vital forces, if they are to work for the one who uses them. In most cases, this renewal of energies is best accomplished by pouring an alcoholic beverage, like whiskey, on the stone, or even by soaking the stone in an alcoholic beverage for some time. Sometimes cold water or oil is to be used, the stone itself will tell you what it requires. I have found that alcohol seems to be more universally preferred by the spirits of most of these stones.

Now the procedure for working with any stone is about the same for all stones. First, a stone is found that has an attraction for the person that wishes to work with it. The attraction is usually mutual between the stone and the person. Then the person enters into conversation with the spirit of the stone, and learns from it what it is that the stone may do, or to put it another way, what powers have been granted to the stone by the creator. Next the person must ask the stone what it would like in return, so that it will freely accomplish what is being asked of it.

With all of this information in hand, the stone is ready to work. The person must now bring the stone home, and there he should wash it, usually in clear cool water. If the stone is dirty, it should be scrubbed thoroughly, using both soap and water. Once the washing is done, and the stone is rinsed and dried, it is usually best if a small preliminary offering of alcohol be given to the stone, to vitalize it for the purpose for which it is to be used. Usually a shot of whisky, that is poured over the stone while it sits in a saucer or in a shallow bowl is sufficient. The stone should be left there for a while, say an hour or so, so that it can absorb the alcohol. Leaving the stone on the saucer with the whisky in contact with it overnight is usually more than enough.

The following day the person should talk to the stone and ask it to do for him what he wants. Then the stone will talk to the person's mind, and explain what it needs in order to do what the person wants. Then the person gets what the stone needs, the stone does what the person wants, and the person rewards the stone with what it wants. Usually the reward is just more whisky.

Although quick to speak of, it may take weeks or months for all of these things to come to fruition. Therefore, the person working with the stone must have patience, as things slowly move along for them. Like everything else on this earth, the results of this work will usually take time to manifest.

Lastly, the person should prayerfully thank God for giving him the stone, and for accomplishing the work that they have asked it to do for you.

Moreover, this is the way in which you may work with stones to help yourself to the glory of God.

Another way you may work with stones is to learn precisely what any given stone you find may do for you. This is done, as is mentioned above by questioning the stone and awaiting the reply. As an example of this, I have a stone in my desk drawer that is more effective than aspirin in removing local pain, such as that of a headache. One day I pinched my fingers in my haste to close a drawer. The stone quickly took the pain away as soon as I passed it over the bruised and sore part of my hand. I thanked the stone, and ran it under cold water to take the pain it had captured away from it. Another stone I found in the street is of assistance in aiding people to meditate, as it helps them blank their mind. A third stone that I found cautions me if the weather will be too inclement. Each of these stones has their own function, but I successfully make use of them all. Just remember that every stone in the entire divine creation has a value that you may discover for yourself if you are attuned to it.

CHAPTER SIX

Understanding Other People

There is a supposed Indian saying that you should not criticize another person until you have walked a mile in their moccasins. While this certainly sounds like a good idea, it would seem that the main difficulty is learning just what you need to know about the other person to understand what their motivations, difficulties, and the other facets of the persons life are. To be brief, the real difficulty is finding the other person's moccasins, so that you can walk in them.

Few people are interested in revealing very much about themselves, and in many cases, what they reveal, even in a formal interrogation, is false information that is actually a lie that the person has told himself about himself. In the case of some people, their true past has been eliminated and completely replaced with a lovely tissue of fantasy, which is as opaque as it can be, often surviving any penetration or casual investigation. Other people seem to be quite open, while actually concealing all of the things they do not wish to admit about themselves, either to themselves, or to others.

How then, can you 'get into the head' of your subject and find out what they are really like, what motivates them and what they actually believe about the various things you are interested in? Well, one way is by investigating the individual using a magic mirror. Using your magic mirror while they are sleeping, you can ask your subject questions that they will answer truthfully in almost all cases. While they are unlikely to lie when questioned by the mirror when they are asleep, in the case of a myth of themselves that they have used so long as to absolutely believe, they invariably will reply to questions based on that myth rather than revealing the objective absolute truth.

You can often penetrate this façade by asking when they began believing this about themselves. If they began to hold this belief after they were about fourteen years old, it is probably a façade of myth. You can then ask them why they beleive this about themselves and often receive more insight into them than you might wish to have. However, this only partially solves the problem.

There has to be a better way to understand other people.

There is a better way, but it requires a very focused mind, one that is free of distractions and chatter, and one that can concentrate quietly and unemotionally for some time. As a magician, you supposedly have developed that kind of mind through the exercises you have been doing. This is a good test for you to see just how effective your mental training has been.

You may perform the following technique either with or without a photograph of the subject. Usually, using a photograph of the subject, at least when you begin doing this technique, is both easier and more effective, as it allows you to focus on the person more directly and specifically. Once you have mastered using a photograph when using this technique, you should try working on someone new without a photograph, just to see how well you do at it. It is entirely possible to do this without a photograph, even when knowing only scanty information concerning the person. However achieving that goal takes a great deal of practice.

Holding the photograph in your hands, focus your mind on the person, while visualizing their mind as if it were a large empty unfurnished room. Once you are completely focused on the person, enter into their mind by seeing yourself inside this room, which you have identified as their mind.

Now patiently wait, the room you have identified as their mind will gradually decorate itself, becoming more and more theirs, and less and less a bare room. When I do this, I visualize the mind I wish to enter as being a huge gymnasium like room with very high ceilings and hardwood floors, well lighted from some source, but with no lights or windows in sight. Once I am 'in' the room, it will quickly decorate itself, becoming the personal mind of the person whom I am trying to learn about. This always takes a few moments, usually it takes considerably more time the first time you investigate a new person. In some few cases, the room will stay empty, and no decorations or other personal objects will appear.

Be patient and allow the room to fill with all of the person's effects. Look at them, but do not think of them, examine them, or comment on them. I might add that you should not be surprised by what you may see either. Some rather conventional looking people have some rather interesting fantasies in the deeper recesses of their mind, the symbols of these fantasies, if not the reality, will often be revealed to you once you enter into their mind in this way.

As you allow the room to gradually fill, look around it dispassionately, observing what is there, but being unconcerned with what you see. At this point, you are only trying to judge when the room has stopped filling with things. Once the room is full, and nothing more is being added, relax yourself in the room.

Now ask your first question, phrasing it in your mind, and then releasing it to the room. In a few moments, you will find that your answer will appear. Be unemotional and dispassionate, regardless of what the answer is. You must be emotionally indifferent to all of this or you will be placing your own values and answers onto your questions, and influencing the answers. You do not need to train you mind to delude yourself in that way.

I might point out here that you must have the questions you wish to ask prepared in advance. Regardless of the answer you receive to the questions, you should only ask the questions you have previously prepared, and you should be careful to not react to any of the answers. Obviously, you should not criticize any of the answers you may receive either. Just accept the answers you receive unemotionally.

Once all of your questions are answered, you may now leave the room, returning to your own space. Now sit and relax for a few seconds, releasing any tension with in you that has resulted from your doing this. Then write out the answers to any of the questions you have had answered. Once you have mastered this technique, you have a sure fire technique for finding out the truth that you seek to know about people.

Some Caveats About Using This Technique

Some people will not allow you into their mind. While these people are in the minority, the sign of this happening is that nothing at all comes into the room of their mind. Your best chance here is to break off the visualization, return to your own space, and use a magic mirror to see what you can get with that. You may also use the mirror to ask the person if you can enter into their mind. In some cases, more often than you might think, you will receive permission from your subject to enter into their mind. If you do gain permission to enter into their mind, things will immediately change in your favor.

Other people, even fewer, will attempt to strike out at anyone trying to enter their mind. Should you suspect that this might occur, use a mirror and ask permission to enter into their mind first. If they deny you permission, ask your question with the person sleeping, using your mirror. Once the question has been asked, it is possible that they will grant you permission to go into their mind. Even the most private and secretive person is more likely to grant you permission to enter their mind when they are asleep. It seems that the sub conscious mind is more open to being friendly, allowing others to speak to it, than the conscious minds of many people are.

In a few cases, even though the 'room of their mind' does not decorate or fill with things, you can still ask questions and receive accurate answers. Wait about three to five minutes for the room to fill, and then begin to ask your questions. You may well receive all of the answers you wish to have from them.

Another System For Attaining The Same Goal

Should you wish, you can simply look at the picture of the person and then visualize yourself just entering into their mind. In some cases this produces better results than visualizing a room, while for other people, the room visualization works better. You can take your choice of these methods. A few people have been able to visualize the other person accurately enough that they do not need to use a photograph. This is a third technique you should try to see if you can make it work for you.

CHAPTER SEVEN

Energy Transfers

Most people are completely open to having their vital energy siphoned off by others. Not only are they open to losing energy in this way, they are frequently unaware that they have lost any energy at all. This interesting fact gives the magician an opening through which they may work with the person to convince them of things that are in favor of the magician, as well as to open the person to the magician in any other way that the magician desires.

The process of draining energy from another person may be either covert or overt. In a covert energy drain, the magician simply consciously draws energy from the other person. The person being drained usually makes no objection to this energy draw, and they are usually consciously unaware of it. Should the magician desire, energy drained out of a person may be replaced with energized thought forms, which will act to convince the person of some truth or guidance information that the magician wants to impart into the person they are draining energy from.

One excellent example of using this replacement technique is in relieving the trauma of withdrawal that the person goes through when quitting smoking. The magician first constructs an energized thoughtform encouraging the person to stop smoking, and including the information that their withdrawal symptoms will not be as great as they might have expected them to be. They next focus on the person and draw energy from them, replacing the energy with the pre made energized thoughtform. In a reasonably short time, the person's determination to stop smoking has been substantially reinforced, while their concern over the effect of any withdrawal symptoms they may feel has been released or at the least eased somewhat. If this is done once or twice a day for the first week or so that the person is going without smoking, they will have substantially less difficulty putting their smoking days behind them.

Other trauma, fears and concerns may be released in the same manner. Another example of this is the fear of surgery. A friend of mine was concerned that if they had a particular surgery they would die. The energy of concern was removed and replaced with a thought form telling them that the operation would be successful, and they would enjoy the recovery experience because they would be away from their daily work. This was done once on each of the two days immediately preceding surgery, and the results were excellent. The person even stated that they were enjoying the vacation from work that their recovery period from surgery had provided them.

Overt draining of energy from another person is done with the permission of the subject. This may be either specific: 'May I draw energy from you for the purpose of helping you stop smoking? Or general, 'May I draw energy from you for purposes of my own?' This permission may be asked either consciously or sub consciously of the subject or through the medium of conversation with the subject in a magic mirror. Either means of granting of permission is equally effective, as the magician now has gained permission to work with the energy of the subject.

There does not seem to be any fundamental difference between the processes of working with someone covertly or overtly using this technique. In either case, the same kind of work is usually being done, and the same results may be expected. It is often thought that in overtly working with someone there is going to be less resistance to any new thoughts that are being given to them. However, this does not seem to bear out in practice, so long as the thoughts being introduced are not emotionally traumatic to the person. I have found that most people seem to accept thoughts equally well, whether or not they consciously say that they wish to have them as a part of their beliefs.

However, if you were to introduce thoughts like, 'you should rob a bank,' or 'you should hit that person,' they are likely to be imposed by the individual's common sense and normal protocols of behavior. When you wish to introduce a thought to another person, regardless of the technique you employ in doing so, you should first think as to how they will react to that thought. This is exactly what you should do in having a normal everyday conversation with the person. There is essentially no difference in introducing a thought to the conscious mind of a person and introducing thoughts to their sub conscious mind. In either case, you should have some idea as to how the person might react to the thoughts you propose to introduce to them. If you introduce disquieting thoughts, you are unlikely to obtain a reasonable response.

Obviously, for a magician, there are any number of ways to determine if the thoughts you intend to introduce are going to be either disquieting or emotionally upsetting to the person. Should you find that the thoughts you wish to introduce would be upsetting, you are far better off not to introduce them. If you have an ultimate thought in mind, it is far better to introduce the thought in stages, usually sib consciously, until you are certain that the ultimate thought will be accepted.

As an example, if 'You are madly in love with Mary Jones' is too strong an initial thought, you could proceed in the following stages:

'Mary Jones is an interesting person.'

'Mary Jones always seems to be _____.' (Bright, cheerful, well dressed, well informed, etc.) "I like people like that.'

'Mary Jones is actually quite pleasant.'

'Mary Jones is pleasant to be around.'

'Mary Jones has some very nice character traits.'

'Mary Jones is someone I would like to know better.'

'Mary Jones would be fun to date.'

'Mary Jones is really a lovely person.'

'Mary Jones would make a good wife and mother.

'Mary Jones is the kind of woman I would like to marry.'

'Mary Jones is someone I could marry.'

'Mary Jones is the kind of woman I would like to spend my life with.'

'Mary Jones is my soul mate, I want to wed her.'

I am madly in love with Mary Jones.'

From the above you can see who is most likely to use this technique in gaining their desires with another. Amatory magic tends to be worked by women.

CHAPTER EIGHT

Developing The Memory

The theory of human faculties is not something that is accepted by modern educators. However, their turning away from this ancient theory of education does not reduce its validity. The theory of faculties states that there are a variety of different faculties in every person, each of which may be developed separately, but all of which work together to make the person a whole human being. As one example, one of these faculties is the faculty of music. Teaching singing develops the music faculty, as does practicing the 'do re me' art known as solfeggio. Once singing and solfeggio have been learned, the theory of music may be taught. In this way, the individual's faculty of music is developed to the greatest possible extent.

Another of the important and very useful faculties is that of memory, which in the one room school house of our early years was taught by the process of requiring the student to learn short verses or poems each day. This practice was started in the earliest grades, and continued to the time of graduation from school. Bible verses, short prayers, and classical aphorisms, such as the Poor Richard aphorisms were initially assigned as memory exercises.

The student was required to master memorizing these shorter tasks, and then go on to memorizing longer phrases, poems and often paragraphs or even pages of text. By the time that most American one-room school students graduated from the sixth grade, they were able to recite the preamble to the Constitution and the Declaration of Independence from memory without any difficulty at all.

The same practice is used today in mastering the art of memory. We begin by memorizing a few lines of text each day, Bible or other religious verses may be used, or the person may select verses from poems, phrases from stories, or the kind of inspiring aphorisms that our ancestors used. During the first year of this work, phrases and stories of twenty-five words or less may be selected, but as these stories are mastered, the person should go on to memorizing longer and longer stories and tales. Longer stories, including those running to four or five pages of printed text might be memorized later on, once there has been a gradual expansion of the ability to of memorize text from one level of memory to another. It is entirely possible for the average person to learn to memorize a seven-page document when reading it twice.

By developing them mnemonic faculty in this way, and by constantly assuring yourself that you have retained all of the information that you have previously memorized, you will gradually expand your mnemonic faculty to the greatest extent possible for you. Once you have reached the capacity of your mnemonic faculty, you will have no difficulty memorizing the words of any magical ritual that you are proposing to perform. Of course, this is only one benefit of your expanded mnemonic development. Your improved memory will allow you to remember many of the other things that you encounter in your daily life, automatically adding them to the store of your memory. As your memory increases, so will your ability to recall what you have learned. These two abilities work hand in hand, greatly expanding your mind.

One of the reasons that many orders and lodges require the candidate to memorize passages of text to prove that they have learned the work required for admission or promotion, is that by placing certain works in the memory, the content of these memorized passages becomes a kind of beacon to the future behavior of the candidate. Subconsciously, you will remember everything that you will ever read over the entire course of your life. When you develop the faculty of your memory, you are developing your ability to consciously recall all of these many memories.

The memorization of uplifting and character building text is an example of a person actually shaping their character by what they read and remember. The words you have read will always have some effect on your life, whether or not you believe that they do. This is a good reason for seriously thinking about what you may chose to read recreationally.

CHAPTER NINE

Making And Using Magic Mirrors

Why Magic Mirrors?

The reason for making and using magic mirrors may not be immediately obvious to the neophyte in the field of the occult arts. While magic mirrors are not difficult to make, they are often quite difficult to learn how to use. Mastering using the magic mirror often requires very difficult and dedicated work on the part of the scryer. While this work develops the concentration and the ability to visualize, as well as assisting in developing the willpower, it may result in the person being able to see only hazy and often obscure images in their mirror. Thus, some people believe that their efforts are in vain, despite the fact that their striving to master the magic mirror has developed within them abilities that will outlast their physical lifetime and will assist them eternally.

Even once using the magic mirror is mastered, it often happens that some practitioners of the occult arts will believe that they will have very little further use for their mirror over the course of time. It often seems that there are a great many more interesting, and even considerably easier or faster means available to provide the information or answer the questions to which the magic mirror can provide solutions. Furthermore, even the best of magic mirror scryers will find that some of the answers they seek may remain hidden from their mirror, although in some cases, these queries may be answered quite readily by other means.

Yet, despite these apparent limitations, the magic mirror is actually one of the most useful of the magician's tools. If it is employed properly, the time and effort spent in mastering its use is well repaid, both in gaining or developing the ability to scry and in many other ways. The overall usefulness and versatility of the magic mirror is actually far greater than that of any other instrument that the magician may use. I believe that it is one of the most useful instruments that a magician may possess. Naturally, I encourage all those who are interested in practical magic to make one, and go on to master the art of using the magic mirror as far as they are able to do so.

Making a Magic Mirror

There have been several books written describing various ways of making magic mirrors. Some of these books describe complex methods of constructing mirrors that would require the services of a skilled wood worker or an even a fine cabinetmaker to complete. Other books describe artful fabrications for magic mirrors that are to be made from rare and costly materials. Magic mirrors of crystal, ivory, emerald, and other expensive materials, as well as those constructed of polished precious metals are frequently mentioned in these tomes. How delightfully romantic, and how absolutely impractical for the average magician or spiritual practitioner such rare and expensive mirrors would be.

While I do not at all doubt that magic mirrors may be constructed from all of these and many other materials, I do not believe that it is necessary to push yourself to the very edge of financial ruin, or even to flirt with bankruptcy to own a magic mirror. In fact, a magic mirror may be made from almost any smooth surface, providing that it is cleaned of unwanted astral influences. It has been my experience that a very useful and quite satisfactory magic mirror may be easily constructed out of simple materials that are widely available to almost everyone. To simplify the entire process of making and using magic mirrors, I recommend that you make a magic mirror by whatever method you wish, as the method by which the mirror is made is actually almost immaterial.

As but one example of this, my former students and I have made a good number of very satisfactory magic mirrors from the kind of inexpensive picture frames with a glass that are sold in variety stores and chain stores. As a quick and inexpensive way to make a magic mirror, I believe that using these picture frames, as the foundation for your mirror has no equal. I shall describe this process for you, so you may make one of these mirrors for your very own.

While I prefer those picture frames that are about eight inches by ten inches in size, magic mirrors are really quite unconcerned with what size they happen to be. I prefer those which are eight by ten inches in size because they are easier to hold, and because my failing eyesight prefers to look at a rather larger image. However, the size of your magic mirror is actually quite unimportant.

Once a suitable picture frame with a glass has been purchased, it is prepared as a magic mirror by first disassembling it and washing all of the non-paper or cardboard parts of the frame and its glass with soap and water. Once the mirror frame and glass have been thoroughly washed, rinsing them in cold water is suggested as the next step. As the backs of these picture frames usually have a cardboard or a heavy paper support for the photograph that is to be inserted by the purchaser, this support must be removed and treated differently than the plastic or wood frame of what is to become your mirror. The frame and glass, once washed and rinsed in cold water, should be well wiped with a cotton ball dipped in a bit of household ammonia. Then the frame and glass should again be rinsed in cold water. This simple washing will usually remove any traces of dirt and grime, as well as removing any stray non-physical influences that may have become attached to the mirror as it made its way from the manufacturers to the store where you purchased it.

I sincerely doubt that anyone goes around attempting to influence these cheap picture frames in the hope that they might later be made into magic mirrors. However, some degree of paranoia seems to be very common among those who practice magic. Thus, if you wish to exorcise the frame or clean it further in some way, you certainly may do so. The choice is yours.

Following the washing, the glass and frame should be allowed to dry in a reasonably neutral atmosphere, at least in a place that has no strong vibrations or heavy emotions of any kind present. Drying the glass and frame in the direct sunlight will usually insure this. Once the mirror and frame are dry, further preparation of it may continue. By the time that the mirror and frame are dry, it may be safely assumed that any stray influences formerly on it have been removed.

Once these stray influences have been removed, we may begin adding our own influences, as well as adding any other influences that we may wish to place on the mirror. We begin to put our own non-physical influence into the mirror by carefully wiping the glass on both sides with a cotton ball soaked in alcohol. Naturally, ethyl alcohol is preferred, but we may use isopropyl-rubbing alcohol if ethyl-rubbing alcohol is unavailable. The purpose of this wiping is to first clean off any alcohol soluble material, as well as to begin to place our own vibration on the mirror. This last is accomplished by using our hand to wipe the mirror with the alcohol swab. Subtle influence it may be, but it is our own influence non-the less. Wiping both sides of the glass accomplishes this quite well. As you wipe the glass with alcohol, you might bear in mind the thought that this glass is to become a magic mirror for you, or for whomever else you may be making it.

Any amount of work we do on anything at all begins to leave some trace of ourselves connected to it. As we will not only be cleaning the glass for our magic mirror but painting it as well, through the work we are doing on the glass we will be leaving a rather substantial trace of ourselves on the finished mirror.

This is one reason why magicians, and other people who work with the non-physical world, often will not allow others, especially strangers, to handle any of the items they use in their work. Magic wands, magic mirrors, tarot cards, and other divination aids, are often kept in hiding, or placed in isolated places, where other people may not either see or touch them. This is done to keep them pure and carrying the influence of their makers, as well as to insure that they are free of influences from others.

We are going to spray paint one side of the glass mirror, and the cardboard back support of the picture frame with black paint. The particular kind or nature of the paint that is used is actually unimportant, but I have found that spray painting gives better results than brushing the paint on, as I never seem to be able to brush paint on glass without leaving a multitude of streaks. For those interested, I use Rust-Oleum black spray paint, which I purchase at a hardware store in my neighborhood. I coat one side of the glass and the mating side of the cardboard backing plate with the paint, and then I allow both of these painted surfaces to dry thoroughly.

Once the paint is dry on both the cardboard and the glass, I apply another coat, and once again allow the paint to dry. I have found that three or four light coats are better than applying one heavy coat of paint that might be liable to run. In a number of cases, I have applied five or six coats of paint, allowing the paint to dry between coats. The object is to produce a completely obscure piece of glass. This means that you cannot see through it. However, you should not have any pinholes of light or other areas of the glass where the paint passes some illumination either. Should these light leaks persist, another coat of paint is usually the best answer.

Allowing the previous coat of paint to dry thoroughly before applying the next coat is also highly advisable. This usually requires waiting at least an hour or more between coats of paint. Once you have sprayed three coats of black paint on ether the cardboard or the glass, you should allow the paint to dry overnight. Spray paint dries rapidly, but it still takes some time to harden completely. An overnight drying is recommended between each application of three coats or more of paint.

Of course, you will only rarely require more than three coats of paint on the cardboard backing material. Three coats of black paint are usually enough for the cardboard. The paint coat renders the cardboard reasonably waterproof and able to last considerably longer that it otherwise would.

The glass may infrequently require more than three coats of spray paint. If you wish to hasten the drying and hardening of the paint, place the glass in a gas oven with the pilot light on for an hour or so. Do not apply heat, as this is more likely to burn the paint, turning what work you have done into a mess that must be scraped away before the glass may be thoroughly cleaned, so you can start all over again.

Once you have a thoroughly black mirror, you may proceed on to the next step. This involves reassembling the picture frame, with the unpainted portion of the glass showing on the finished mirror. Once this has been accomplished, your magic mirror is ready for you to begin to use.

Consecrating your Mirror

There are numerous spells and rituals of consecration for the magic mirror, some of which are to be repeated each time the mirror is used. If you believe that any of these are necessary, then they are necessary for you. You should use the consecration ritual of your choice to consecrate your magic mirror.

On the other hand, if you do not believe that such rituals are necessary, they are not necessary for you. In fact, the time and effort that you have put forth in making your own magic mirror has made it yours, and for that reason alone, it is rarely necessary to go through a special consecration ritual to have the mirror harmonized with you. Once you have begun working with the mirror, your effort will make it even more yours, as you will be putting even more effort and energy into it as you use it.

You can now go on to learn how to see in your magic mirror. Frankly, this is the most difficult part of the work for most people. As with all else in magic, patient and dedicated effort will see you through.

Learning to Use Your Magic Mirror

Before you begin working with your magic mirror, you should find about a half hour of time each day during which you will not be disturbed. You will need to reserve this time, setting it aside to devote to learning how to use your magic mirror. You must also announce to your family, roommates, and friends, that you will simply not be available to them during this time. Working with a magic mirror requires a great deal of focus and concentrated effort. This dedication of time and focus of intent seems to be something to which many people do not seem to be able to commit themselves. Unless you can dedicate this time to mastering your magic mirror, you will not likely be very successful in learning to use it.

Your magic mirror is not a television set. Please bear this in mind. When you first begin using it, you cannot command it to show an image and assume that it will reveal the exact image you desire to see in full motion and living color. Once you have mastered the use of the magic mirror, you will be able to follow the actions of the persons you are interested in as they go through their daily affairs. However, becoming sufficiently proficient with the magic mirror to accomplish this takes a great deal of time, as well as many hours of practice. Even then, it will never become a kind of occult television receiver that you may use to present you with all of the images, past present and future, of both the physical and non-physical realms that you may desire to peer into solely for curiosity's sake.

What you actually will be able to eventually see in any magic mirror is always dependent on your personal capacity to use a magic mirror. In this, as in all else, not all people are alike. Some surprising people, including some who are seemingly indifferent to either the occult or the non-physical world, are far more gifted at using a magic mirror than are other people who may be dedicated and hard working students of the occult arts. Your goal should be to develop yourself to the furthest limit of your capacity, not to be concerned with what you discover that your capacity may happen to be. As in all else found in dealing with the non-physical arts and sciences, development of the psychic or non-physical senses are not ever a competitive sport.

It may not seem at all obvious, but the first thing to be mastered in learning to use a magic mirror is simply learning to hold it in your hands. You will be looking into this mirror for what may be an hour or more at a time. In many cases, you will wish to write something, or to hold the mirror with one hand while you do something else with the other. This requires that you first get used to holding the mirror at what is a comfortable viewing angle for you. Then you must accustom yourself to manipulating it, by shifting it from one hand to the other, using your free hands while holding the mirror, and so forth. You must master the art of dealing with the mirror just as you would actually do in a normal working session with your magic mirror. Magic mirrors that hang on walls are very nice, but it is also possible to get neck or back strain from using them. A hand held magic mirror is much more practical, and is just as effective.

Incidentally, I have never seen a talking magic mirror, such as is featured in Walt Disney's movie, 'Snow White.' A mirror of this kind would have to have an active spirit attached to it. This is something that is quite far from anything we are discussing in this book.

Practice the holding and manipulation of your magic mirror for at least a week during the half-hour's time each day that you have devoted to learning to use your magic mirror. You can do this while you firmly establish among the various members of your household, that you are quite sincere about your not wishing to ever be disturbed during this dedicated time. If possible, turn off your telephone and ignore or silence the doorbell as well during the time you have dedicated to mastering the magic mirror.

Your body should be relaxed and your mind calm, but in these first sessions, you should not attempt to do anything other than become acquainted with holding your magic mirror. As you practice this, please bear in mind that you are not trying to see anything at all. You are just trying to accept the mirror, and become comfortable holding it and looking into it. Your only goal with this exercise is to become acquainted with the process of holding your mirror and looking into it.

Should you believe this first exercise to be idle, you will soon find that the process of just holding the mirror will be one that will interfere with your eventual attempt to see images in it. Both your body and your mind must be thoroughly trained to perform any new task that you undertake. Once you are accustoming to holding the mirror, the physical changes brought about by holding it can be placed into the background of your mind. Then you will be able to concentrate both body and mind on actually doing the following exercises in this series, and learning to see things in the mirror.

When you have finished using your magic mirror at the end of the time you have set aside for this exercise, you should put it away in a safe place. My students who made their mirrors from inexpensive picture frames, all made small pillowcase like covers, which slipped over them. Most of my students kept their completed mirrors hidden in their dressers in their bedrooms. I have always kept my magic mirrors in cardboard or wooden boxes. I separate them by placing a larger piece of cardboard between them.

While you are working on mastering the first exercise, you should prepare yourself for the next. You may do this by having on hand a photograph of a scene with which you are familiar. A photograph of your back yard, or of the front of your home is ideal. The photograph should not contain any people or animals. It should be a photograph only of scenery and buildings. If you wish, you may take this photograph especially for the purpose of this exercise. Study this photograph for four or five minutes each day, following the time you have spent holding your magic mirror. Do not consciously attempt to memorize this photograph, simply view it as you hold it in front of you. As you do this, your body should be relaxed and your mind calm, just as it was when you held your magic mirror earlier. Your goal with this exercise is only to become thoroughly familiar with this photograph.

After the week you have spent becoming used to holding and manipulating your mirror, it is time for you to go on to the meat of the matter, viewing images in the mirror. To begin to do this, first prepare yourself by sitting with the mirror in your hands, the photograph you have been looking at out of sight. Now relax your physical body, and after calming yourself, concentrate on the mirror. Then visualize the image on the photograph, just as if you were seeing it on the surface of the mirror. Do this with a certain amount of emotional indifference, as if it were unimportant to you whether you saw an image or not. At the same time, you should look at the mirror as if the most important thing in the world was what you were seeing in the mirror, regardless of what that image might be.

Call up as clear an image of the picture you have been looking at as you can, calling it into your mind. Now see this image as if it were projected on the glass surface of your magic mirror. Depending on your ability to concentrate and visualize, this image may be sharp or fuzzy, or you may still see it only in your mind. Do not be concerned about this. Simply visualize the image you seek on the glass of the mirror. Concentrate on this image for at least five minutes.

The first time you do this, you are quite likely to say that it is impossible. However, it is not only possible, it is something that many people have accomplished in the past, people with no more natural ability than you have. However, mastering this art requires a particular tweak of the mind to accomplish. Unless you have already mastered that mental 'tweak' somehow, you will probably have some difficulty seeing the image you desire to see. Practice for five minutes, and then take a five-minute break. Then return, and practice visualizing the image you desire to see again. Once again, try for five-minutes and take another five-minute break. In this way, work through your first practice session of half an hour.

To be very frank, only a very few people can accomplish seeing an image in a magic mirror the first time they try it. The odds are greatly against your mastering this technique in your first four or five sessions. If you understand that it takes time, and effort, you will be able to do much better, when you do finally master that mental 'tweak' of the mind, which allows you to see images in your magic mirror.

One of the reasons that I recommend half hour sessions, and break them down into five-minute practice and five minutes of break is that until you are facile with the magic mirror, you should not strain yourself using it. Using the magic mirror for any long length of time, especially when you are new to using it, can cause your mind to drift into the fantasy land of what you wish to see in the mirror, rather than viewing what is actually there to be seen in the mirror.

Just as in all of my other writings, I again caution you here against falling into self-delusion, that ever-present enemy of the real magician. Self-delusion is that which causes the deluded magician to perform magical miracles that exist only in their mind. Over use of the magic mirror, using it for more than an hour at a setting can cause this self-delusion to appear, distorting what you are actually seeing into the fantasy of what you might wish to see. Once you have perfected yourself in the use of the magic mirror, you can use it for an hour at a time, but that takes at least a year or a year and a half's successful practice using the mirror in interrupted experiences over a half hour at a time.

If you practice seeing the picture in the mirror each day for a week, a half hour at each session, interrupted as directed above, you will probably begin to see at least the outline of the major constituents of the photograph that you have previously studied. You must not afflict yourself by imposing any self-imposed judgments as to what you see, or any self derived time schedule. Just practice the exercise as directed, and do not be concerned whether you are practicing this exercise correctly or not.

It is very important to avoid having any emotional reaction to what you see in your magic mirror. You must neither criticize yourself for not seeing what you desire to see, nor congratulate yourself for seeing something that you may desire to see. Neither must you correct yourself for seeing an incomplete image. Simply see what you see, and placidly accept what you see. You must avoid making any emotional judgments at all about what you see or do not see in your magic mirror.

Every person performing this exercise will have quite variable results with it. One day you may find that you see all of the details of the image sharp and clear, while the following day you may see only a barely recognizable fuzzy outline of the image. You will have days when you see a barely recognizable fuzzy shape, and other days when you see nothing at all. You must realize that this variability in your results is perfectly normal. Do not allow this variability to concern you, and most especially, do not criticize yourself because of the great variability in the results you are achieving.

You must further realize that there is nothing odd about your being able to see images in a magic mirror. This ability is a normal human ability, but unfortunately one that our present materialistic society has turned against in its drive to reduce everything in the universe to a matter of material objects and physical gadgets. You are certainly not using your magic mirror through the agency of spirits or other non-physical creatures either. You are accomplishing the task of seeing in a magic mirror through the cooperation of your physical and non-physical selves. No outside influence is ever needed for anyone to make use of a magic mirror.

You should perform this exercise at least a half hour each day for at least a month or more. Always strive to see what the photograph shows, but do so without any desire for accomplishment, and without any self-criticism for falling below your expectations. You should never fear to fail at any of the very many psychic development exercises you may attempt. You will find that as time passes, your results will usually be quite variable, but if you persist, you will eventually consistently succeed at what you are attempting. You will not be progressing linearly, seeing increasingly clear images and having better vision in your magic mirror each day. Do not be discouraged, as perseverance is what eventually conquerors in this art, as it does in all other matters dealing with the non-physical realms.

By the end of two weeks practice, you will usually be able to see at least an outline, hazy and indifferent though it may be. On the other hand, you may see only a line or two of the image that you are seeking.

While you are seeking an image, discouraging thoughts may come up in your mind, turning you away from your effort. In some cases, you will probably wish to make note of these discouraging thoughts and de-energize their hold on you once your practice session with your magic mirror is finished. Keeping a paper and pencil at hand is a good way to make note of these discouraging thoughts.

Should you be able to see a moderately clear image, then you must strive to ever increase your ability to see in the mirror with increasing clarity. This is a matter of long practice, and not something that may be developed immediately. You should persist in your efforts until you are consistently able to see an image just as sharp and clear as the photograph that you originally used as your target. While it is obvious that some people will develop to be better scryers with a mirror than others, you must realize that everyone can master using their magic mirror to at least some extent. Your only task is only to strive to do the very best you can, to become the best scryer that you can be.

Once you can see an outline of the photograph, this is not the time to decide that since you can see at least a recognizable image in the mirror you will now turn your attention to viewing scenes other than the photograph you have been using. You must work with the photograph until you are absolutely certain that you can see it no more clearly than you now do. After at least a years practice with the mirror, and two or three weeks with no improvement, but with a consistent clear and sharp image in your mirror, it will be all right if you decide to stop trying to improve your skill.

Then you should go on to viewing another photograph of the same kind, one of a scene without people or animals in it. These scenes are best, as they usually carry no surprises once you switch from seeing the image on the photograph, to viewing the scene as it presents itself to you today.

You should save work that is more complex for the time
when you have perfected yourself in using your mirror. That
time will eventually come, and then you will be able to do what
you wish about viewing those things that you desire to see in
your mirror. For now, you must simply continue to develop
yourself and master the art of seeing in your magic mirror.

The next step is to be taken once you have mastered obtaining
a clear and sharp image in your magic mirror. Then you will
begin a practice session by forming a clear and sharp image in the
mirror, and ask to see the image of that scene as it is now, rather
than as it was when the photograph you have been using was
taken. You should immediately see the image of the scene as it is
at present, including seeing any people or animals that may now
be present in the scene. You may now study this scene, continuing
to refine your perceptions of what you see. Often mastering this
takes several dozen additional practice sessions, while sometimes
it requires another six months or more to perfect. Once you have
mastered seeing the image of your photograph as it currently is,
you may go on to looking at other things, should you desire to
do so.

The reason that we do not use a picture or an image of a
person or animal in developing our abilities with the mirror is
that when you are just beginning, the sub conscious desire to
identify the person or animal takes precedence over learning to
see the image itself. This is a natural human instinct, which often
blocks the developing scryer from seeing the image properly. By
using a picture that has no image of a human or animal in it, we
avoid that difficulty all together.

A Few Cautions And Some Guidance In Using The Mirror

There are a few cautions that you should observe concerning
requesting to see or view things in your magic mirror. Firstly,
you should always ask to view the spirit of anyone who either is
or who may be deceased. If you do not specify that you wish to

see the spirit, you will possibly get the body, which can be rather shocking if you are not used to looking at the bodies of people in various stages of decomposition.

Next, you probably know or have heard that you can summon functional parts of living people into your magic mirror. This is something that is always far more successful when the people are asleep than it is when they are awake. However, before you summon someone into your mirror, you should always ask to view him or her, to see if they are either asleep or awake. While you are viewing them, you can ask them if they are willing to allow you to summon them into your mirror. In a surprising number of cases, people are most willing to be summoned into a magic mirror.

If the person you wish to call into your mirror agrees to be summoned, you may then just ask them to come into your mirror, and as they do so, state firmly to them that they will always respond to your summons as quickly and as easily as they did this time. This will make future summonings of the same person considerably easier for you.

Should you wish to see someone in your mirror, you can see what he or she is presently doing, or has been doing over the last few weeks. You may accomplish that simply by asking, in your thoughts, to see what they have been doing at such and such a time. The image of their activity, past or present, will present itself to you.

Usually it is increasingly difficult to go back beyond a month or so in the life of a person, and view their actions. However, if they have had a traumatic experience in the past, it may be possible to view that experience no matter how long ago it happened. This difficulty comes about because the memory you are seeking is dependent upon the emotional energy that the person had invested in that memory at the time it occurred. Some people ordinarily place a great deal of emotion in what others might consider to be trivial memories, while other people place very little emotion into any of their memories.

Which condition a particular person follows may not be accurately prejudged in advance. You will have to attempt to see these things in your mirror for yourself. You will either be able to see certain things in the person's past, or you will find that there is so little emotional energy placed in them that they could not successfully be viewed in your mirror.

Viewing locations, scenes, landscapes, and so forth is accomplished in the same manner. You simply ask with your mind to see what you wish to see. The view will then present itself in the mirror. In many cases, you will find that you may be able to see what you ask for from the eyes of a living human being who is currently witnessing the scene. Otherwise, you may see the scene in some other way, usually as an emotional memory.

You must recall that the time of day is quite different in other parts of the world. One of my students kept looking for his ancestors' home after supper every night, only to tell me that there was never any light there. In fact, he was looking at a place when it was always quite dark, because the sun had set, and the place the ancestors home was located was not illuminated after sun set. Once he looked for the location after breakfast on the weekend, he had much better luck finding it.

It is always very important for you to apply common sense to any question that you seek to answer before you try to solve it using either physical divination or non-physical scrying. These means of answering questions should be reserved for those things that cannot be answered logically in the physical world.

Once you have mastered using the magic mirror, you may now see and learn. Your mirror is now yours to command.

Some Practice Exercises With The Magic Mirror

1. —Take some time watching the street outside a window. See it physically, and then look at the same scene in the magic mirror. Observe any differences that you may see. Gradually bring the image in the mirror into line with what you physically see when looking out of your window.

This is very much like seeing the astral realms on the street, which you must master when learning the projection of the non-physical body from the physical body. You must learn to clearly see what is physically present, while ignoring things that you see which exist only in the non-physical realms.

2. —Look at a bus or a taxicab. Try to follow that bus or cab in your magic mirror as it travels around the city. Do not do this exercise for more than a half hour at a time. Remember that taxicab drivers often work twelve-hour shifts. You only need to follow the cab for a half hour.

3. —If friend or lover is going to the store, follow their activities in your magic mirror. Tell them you will be doing this in advance, and make notes of what you see. Discuss what you saw with your friend after they return.

4. —If you have a friend going to a different city as on a business trip, follow them on their air flight and arrival at the airport.

5. —Attempt to look at people you knew in the past. Fellow school students and similar former friends and acquaintances will provide a good selection of those you might wish to call into your mirror and learn about. Make note of those whom you believe are still active, and attempt to find their address and write them. See if you can confirm their location with what you saw in your magic mirror.

Fluid Condensers

Once you have mastered the art of seeing an image in the black magic mirror, the process may be simplified considerably by using what are know as a fluid condensers. These materials attract and hold influences of the non-physical world, or what is usually referred to as the astral world. When you project an image from your mind onto a surface that is coated with a fluid condenser, the fluid condensed receives this image and allows it to strengthen and form the non-physical thought image you have projected into a more complete image of what it is that you wish to see.

Now you might think that it would make the entire process of seeing things in a magic mirror much simpler, if you had just used a fluid condenser from the beginning. This is not true, just as learning to walk using crutches does not actually give an advantage to anyone. Those who can walk only with crutches soon become impossible to separate from their crutches. They are now tied to their crutches so they can walk. Those who learn to scry in a magic mirror with a fluid condenser never become as proficient at their art as those who learn to scry in a plain black mirror. This is the reason I urge you to master scrying in the black mirror first. Once you master that art, you may find that scrying in a mirror that has been coated with a fluid condenser has become simplicity itself.

While the fluid condenser that you use must be one that harmonizes with the individual using the mirror that is not ever such a restriction as one might believe. Almost all people may use Calendula or Marigold flower tea as a fluid condenser. Certain quite exceptional people may be able to use grease or butter stains on ordinary paper to read the astral influences from, but they are the exception. Reading the astral influences from a mirror coated with calendula tea is far more common. Other people may find that they can best read astral impressions from fluid condensers of a different kind. As with everything else in magic, you must find what works best for you, and use that.

Another consideration is that different fluid condensers respond best to different astral influences. Those looking into current events and the past of the physical world will usually find that Calendula tea will do quite well for them. Those who are interested in exploring the non-physical realms may find that other fluid condensers will serve better for their purposes.

You may often find that magicians have several magic mirrors, each attuned to different areas of the physical or the non-physical world. One mirror generally tuned to the physical world, and one mirror generally tuned to the non-physical world is certainly useful for any magician. This tuning of the mirrors is gained by using different fluid condensers on the two mirrors.

Making Simple Fluid Condensers

Simple fluid condensers are made from one herb. Complex fluid condensers, made of two or more herbs, or of combinations of other ingredients, are best left to Alchemists to make. Making them is considerably more complex than the kitchen chemistry task of making simple fluid condensers.

The herbs most frequently used for making simple fluid condensers are, beginning with everyone's favorite, Marigold or Calendula Flowers, then Camomile, Chinese black tea, White Lilly blossoms, Poplar tree leaves, Mandragora roots, and Arnica Montana Flowers. I have heard of other herbs being used as fluid condensers, but I have had no experience using them. Should you wish to 'search the literature' for additional fluid condensers, I would suggest that you first look at the books of Franz Bardon. There are other writers who mention these astral condensers, but Mr. Bardon seems to me to have been the best informed about them. However, you should try a number of these condensers, and see which one works best for you. That is my recommendation in all cases.

The herbs I have listed above are those I have had the best results with, although I usually use Calendula, which I highly recommend to you. The procedure I use in making a fluid condenser from any of these herbs is as follows.

First, I begin with a hand full or a measuring cup full of the herb, (Flower, chopped root, or leaf) either dried or fresh. I place the herb in an iron pot with about two cups of water covering it. Close the pot by putting on the lid, and allow the herb to steep in the water for about two hours before heating the pot. Ideally, the herb should be completely covered by the water. If this is not the case, add another cup or so of water.

Once the herbs are thoroughly wet, place the pot over a low heat, and allow the liquid to simmer for between at least twenty minutes to an hour, or even longer if you wish. Be sure not to boil the liquid, and especially, do not allow it to boil vigorously. The purpose of this heating is to extract the essence of the herb into the liquid. The 'harder' or drier the herb, the more simmering is required. Thus, barks, roots, and dry leaves, need to be simmered quite a bit longer than either flowers or green leaves.

Once the herb has simmered long enough, remove the pot from the fire and without removing the lid, allow the pot to come to room temperature. When the mixture has reached room temperature, strain out the herbs.

The herbs may now be set to soak in about a half cup of alcohol. Ethyl drinking alcohol is preferred, but Alcohol made from Vodka is almost equally satisfactory. Do not soak the herbs in ethyl rubbing alcohol, as it has other things added to it that will cause you to lose much of the benefit of the mixture.

Place the liquid water mixture, or tea, back on the heat and bring it to a low simmer again. Keep the liquid at a low simmer until the volume of the liquid is reduced from whatever you started with to about a quarter of a cup or less. The lower the heat you can obtain this reduction at, the better quality of product you will obtain. You should check this reduction at least every hour, as you slowly allow it to progress. In some cases, it may be necessary to move the liquid to another, smaller, vessel as the reduction occurs.

Once the mixture is reduced in volume, again allow it to cool to room temperature with the lid on the pot. Now add an amount of the alcohol that you have been soaking the herbs in equal to about a quarter of the volume of the liquid, or even a bit less. This product is the finished mixed simple fluid condenser.

Personalizing your fluid condenser is accomplished by adding a drop either of your blood, semen, menstrual blood, or vaginal lubrication. Once it is personalized, you may add about ten drops of homeopathic gold tincture, which serves to protect the mixture from negative non-physical influences.

Stir the mixture thoroughly for a few minutes, and then filter the entire mixture into a dropper bottle, which must be kept tightly closed when not in use. This is the completed fluid condenser. Please remember that it must be thoroughly shaken before each use. To use the condenser, place five or six drops of the fluid condenser on cotton ball, and coat the glass of your magic mirror with the fluid. Allow it to dry, and your magic mirror has been treated with your fluid condenser.

Making a Homeopathic Gold Tincture Useful for Fluid Condensers

Dissolve one metallic gold 1M homeopathic tablet in no more that two teaspoons (1/2 oz) of distilled or purified water. Shake and dissolve the tablet, and the tincture is prepared. Use the tincture within a month or discard it. This gold tincture may be refrigerated and kept for up to three months or so if desired. It has few other uses than protecting fluid condensers, as far as I know. Making it may be a task assigned to one person in a group, so that the tincture may be shared by all of the members of a group, if that is desired.

Making Ethyl Alcohol from Vodka

In some states in the United States, it is impossible to purchase tax paid Ethyl Alcohol. Alchemical alcohol made from wine, whether single distilled (1X), or triple distilled (3X) is also often impossible to obtain. When you require ethyl alcohol, for whatever purpose, you may make it from vodka, which is usually available everywhere that alcoholic liquors are sold.

To find the percentage of alcohol in the vodka, divide the proof in half. 80 proof vodka is 40% alcohol. Alchemical alcohol is graded differently, as it is usually graded by the number of distillations, 1X for single distilled, 2X for double distilled and 3X for triple distilled. The old 600 proof for triple distilled, 400 proof for double distilled and 200 proof for single distilled is hardly ever found anymore.

Purchase a quart or larger bottle of vodka of the highest proof available in the liquor store. 80 proof or 40 % alcohol is reasonably common, but you can occasionally find 100 proof, or 50% alcohol vodka. Pour out a cup of the vodka into another container. The purpose of removing it from the bottle is to allow for the expansion of the water when we freeze the liquid in the bottle. Now set your freezer low, at a point where ice cream stays very hard. If you have a thermometer in your freezer, set the freezer for about 28 degrees or below.

Place the bottle of Vodka, lying on its side in the freezer for at least an hour or two. You will notice that ice will form inside the bottle. Once the amount of ice in the bottle has stabilized, and does not seem to be increasing, take the bottle of Vodka out of the freezer and pour the liquid remaining in the bottle into a third clean container. Do not pour it into the container into which you put the cup of vodka from the full bottle.

The liquid you pour out of the vodka bottle is primarily alcohol. Now you can place this third container in the freezer, and leave it over night. In the morning, pour out the liquid alcohol.

The water that froze in the freezer can be consolidated in the original vodka bottle, along with the cup of vodka you took from the bottle. You may now use this as your 'private stock' drink, should you wish to do so. It should have a very low alcohol content.

The alcohol that you have removed from the vodka will usually have an alcohol content of between 75% to 90% alcohol. This means that it will burn if you light it. This alcohol is strong enough to use in making magic mirrors, as well as for almost any other magical purpose for which you may wish to use it.

I am aware that some purists prefer to use alcohol made Alchemically. This is alcohol that is distilled from (usually) red wine, the wine being made from ripe grapes, it is a far more natural and 'live' product than the alcohol used in making vodka, which is only rarely distilled from any vegetable product. Personally, I would prefer to use alchemical alcohol myself, except that it is prohibitively expensive. Unless you make your own grape wine and then distill the alcohol, I am afraid that the cost of the finished product of the alchemist is beyond the means of any but the most well off.

Should you happen to know an alchemist who makes alchemical alcohol, you might ask him if he makes fluid condensers as well. If so, you will probably find it less expensive, and certainly less time consuming, to purchase the fluid condensers from him than to make them yourself.

Another product that makes a useful fluid condenser is Homeopathic Calendula succus. This is an alcoholic mixture of calendula made by the homeopathic pharmacist. It may be purchased mail order from some homeopathic pharmacies, and is about as useful a fluid condenser as you can find for sale in stores.

Calendula succus is used in the same manner as any other fluid condenser, being applied to a cotton ball and rubbed over the surface of your magic mirror. Once dry, you have an excellent fluid condenser that you should find most useful for investigating the physical world.

Some Interesting Explorations With Magic Mirrors

Once you have had a year or more experience using a magic mirror, you have probably been able to see all of the interesting sights that you wished to see. Now it is time to enter into the realm of exploring those things that you might not have thought of, or had thought of, but possibly did not think could be accomplished with your magic mirror.

Many magicians wish to work with goetic spirits or those of the lower astral. These spirits may be summoned into a magic mirror, just as the spirits or images of living human beings can be summoned. However, it is necessary to note that you should take all of the ordinary ceremonial magical protective precautions before you do so. It may not seem obvious, but even work on the higher astral planes can be both dangerous and disconcerting to the magician. Because of this, using a circle and doing formal sealing and banishing when called for is a necessity when working with any of these spirits.

The authority for this work is Carol 'Poke' Runyon, of the

O.T.A. You may contact them through C.H.S. Publications, PO Box 403, Silverado, California 92676. They have numerous publications, some of which deal with summoning spirits into a magic mirror.

Working with living humans in a magic mirror is quite easy, as is working with the spirits of the reasonably together dead. This is especially true of those whom you knew when they were alive. In the latter case, you may be able to resolve any issues that you had with them, and communicate with them on a fairly warm and friendly level. Just do not expect that a deceased friend or relative has become marvelously spiritual, or is suddenly very knowledgeable about the details of the other world.

This is not to say that you cannot have a good time playing around with magic mirrors. Your explorations are limited only by your imagination, but you should be certain that you avoid falling into the ever-present trap of self-delusion and fantasy, which is ever ready to claim the errant and self-involved magician.

I mentioned in my book '*Mental Influence*' that it is possible to hypnotize someone using a magic mirror. If this is done when the person is asleep, they usually will awaken with no memory of being influenced at all, and with the suggestions, you have implanted in them firmly in place. This technique is an excellent way to assist people to cease smoking or drinking, as well as persuade them to do other things you wish them to do, so long as they are not out of the realm of possibility for them, and do not conflict with their personal ethics or beliefs.

This is an excellent way to help those who say that they wish to rid themselves of a bad habit. I recommend my book '*Mental Influence*' to you for further information on this topic, but I suggest that you learn to hypnotize others first, if you have not already learned to practice that very useful art.

There are a number of interesting variations that you can practice with magic mirrors, once you have mastered the basic art of seeing into the mirror. You might wish to try one or more of the following to expand your magical techniques, and take your use of magic mirrors to a new level.

Enlivening Photographs

A grandmotherly lady of my acquaintance has photographs of her three children and five grand children hanging on the wall of her living room. All of these photographs continually report on the activities of the people whose photographs they are. She explained to me that they rarely write to her, so she uses this technique to keep in touch with them.

This is accomplished by coating the photographs evenly with a thin coating of calendula succus. The photographs are then allowed to dry, and replaced in their frames, which have had the glass wiped with alcohol and ammonia to remove any dirt, as well as any odd or negative influences. If desired, a prayer may be made over the photograph, calling a reflection of the person's current activities into the frame. My acquaintance uses this simple trick to keep track of her far-flung family.

A student of mine who had a four-year relationship break off quite suddenly, and to her great surprise, used a somewhat more investigative application of this technique. She had become more that just proficient in the use of the magic mirror, and after investigating the young man with her mirror; she decided to monitor his activities on a continuous basis. She charged the glass covering a small picture frame containing an illustration and a poem to report on the doings of her former lover. As he went through his daily activities, the mirror showed him doing so. From time to time, she would look into the mirror and 'check up' on his activities. Naturally, her former lover did not know he was being so closely watched, and there was no photograph of him in her apartment to give anyone any suspicion that she was still interested in him.

She obtained a great deal of information concerning her former lover and his new girl friend from this dedicated magic mirror. This information included the fact that his current girl friend had begun a sexual relationship with her former lover a year before he had separated himself from her.

My student used the information she received from the mirror to her advantage by attacking her former lover and his new girl friend magically. Naturally, once the relationship between the two of them had been destroyed, she refused to take her former lover back, as he had confidently expected that she would. The situation being solved to her satisfaction, she thoroughly washed the picture frame containing the illustration and poem, putting the man permanently out of her life.

Once you master the art of using the magic mirror, and become sufficiently adept with it, it becomes possible to use almost any surface you wish to obtain the information you desire. To do this, you should use a fluid condenser on the surface you wish to use as a mirror. To make an ordinary glass surface into a magic mirror, simply coat it with a light coat of the fluid condenser of your choice. If you wish to have it become a reporting mirror, as previously mentioned, just pray over the coated surface stating exactly what you wish to see in it. For the purpose mentioned in the previous example, a typical prayer might be:

> "I pray that this mirror revel to me the current doings and activities of *N. N.*, my former boy friend, so that I may assure myself of his true interest in me."

Naturally, the image projected into a magic mirror that is dark and well made will be quite different from the image projected into the clear glass covering a picture or a photograph of an entirely different subject. It takes a bit of effort to see the image floating on the fluid condenser coating the surface of the picture or photograph, and differentiate the non-physical image from the physical image of the photograph or picture. However, once you have mastered the use of the magic mirror, this differentiation is considerably easier to make.

Applying the fluid condenser directly to the photograph means that you will have to wash it off the photograph, should you wish to rid yourself of the non-physical image. This will usually leave the photograph in rather poor condition, so unless you have facilities for repairing these photographs, I suggest that you coat the glass of the frame in which the photograph resides. Naturally, if it is a photograph of your children or grand children you will probably not ever wish to cease viewing their activities.

Portable Magic Mirrors

Over the years, several versions of portable magic mirrors have been presented to me. The three varieties of portable magic mirrors I have found most useful are presented below in the chronological order in which I first made use of them. I have found them all reasonably useful, although the first is somewhat more useful for women than for men.

1.   —Coat the mirror in a pocket compact after removing the powder that usually comes in the compact. The mirror may be replaced with black glass, coated with a fluid condenser if desired. This makes a convenient and easy to carry portable magic mirror.
2.   —Make a black mirror by coating the inside of a small tin box, like the metal cigarette boxes that are used for expensive cigarettes. Once the painted surface dries, it may be coated with the fluid condenser of your choice. If you wish, you can paint and coat both the inside top and bottom, and thus have two magic mirrors. In this case, you should use a piece of white cardboard to separate the two mirrors.
3.   —You can make a paper magic mirror by coating a small piece of black paper, say business card size, up to three inches by five inches. Coating the paper with a fluid condenser makes the mirror. When dry, the paper may be carried in your purse or pocket wallet. When you need to refer to the mirror, you may bring it out for your use.

CHAPTER TEN

The Magic of Earth

Dirt collected from different places have the vibration or essence of the place from where they originate. This vibration or essence may be put to use magically, should you desire to do so. There are several different approaches to this magic, one of which is used to send annoying people away from you. We will discuss this interesting technique first.

Getting Rid Of Someone

Usually, when you wish to rid yourself of someone, you only want him or her permanently out of your sight. If you have a neighbor whose obnoxious behavior had gone far beyond what you can tolerate, you might think about sending them away from your home in Ohio. You mighty believe that their finding a permanent residence in Florida or Alabama might be good for them. If you can get some dirt from either of the places you wish to send the obnoxious one, your wishes have a good chance of being filled.

Take about a cup of dirt from the place you wish to send the obnoxious person, and divide it into two piles. Place a piece of paper with the names of the person and all of the members of their family you wish to move written on it inside of one of these piles of dirt. (You can use young child #1, etc. if you don't know their names.) Now, with the two piles standing next to each other, pray sincerely over them that the person and all of the members of his family on the paper move to the place from where you obtained the dirt, and that they be happy there, with no desire to ever return to visit their old home. If you wish, you can add power to the prayer by lighting a candle or two before you make the prayer.

Once the prayer has been made, and the candles if any were used have burned out, you now place the dirt with the names in it, in an envelope or plastic 'baggie.' The other pile of dirt is to be cast in their yard, on their porch, or in front of their door. In many cases, the person will be transferred to that location, or they may find a far better job opportunity there, necessitating a move. I mention this to assure anyone performing this spell that the move is not always a disaster for the person who is being magically relocated.

Using Collected Earths

Collected earths or dirt's maybe obtained from any number of places. A bit of dirt from a crossroads can be used to confuse someone, by opening up too many choices for them to make. It also may be used to help someone gain an opportunity. The following is just one example of a spell using collected dirt's. There are probably hundreds of others.

Collect about a teaspoon of dirt from the intersection of two or more roads. An example would be dirt swept from the center of a crossroads when there is a lull in the traffic. Write the name of the person who is to be confused on a piece of paper, and place some of the dirt over it. Now twist the ends of the paper together, so that the paper holds the dirt inside, against the name of the person to be confused. Now make a prayer over the paper that the person be unable to make up their mind and, and that he cannot come to a decision. You can stress the particular thing or issue that you are interested in should you wish. Seal the ends of the paper, and the seam with a piece of tape, and then place the wrapped paper away where you can find it when or if you wish to undo it.

Dirt from a prison may make a person feel as if they are confined. There is an old prison in Philadelphia that frequently takes people on tours. It is an excellent source of prison dirt. Any other prison is of the same character, as dirt may be taken from the visitor's waiting room. This room is usually open to the public during visitor's hours. For a small consideration, prison guards can also provide you with this dirt.

Following the same procedure as given above, except your prayer should indicate that the person should feel confined, as if they have lost their freedom for whatever reason you desire to tell them of. For example, since their engagement or marriage, since they have been living with so and so, since they have left you, or whatever you may desire. As you can see, this spell is very useful in the preliminaries when working toward breaking up a relationship.

Dirt from a church can be used to give a person guilty feelings about their religion, as well as to encourage then to follow a more religious life.

Dirt from the steps of a building can be used to encourage a person to enter that building. This is useful in encouraging someone to file a lawsuit, or even to go on to college.

Dirt from a high traffic area, such as a downtown shopping area, can be used to encourage people to shop in a store. Sprinkle this dirt in front of the store that is to have increased traffic, with a little of the dirt going inside the store.

Dirt from graveyards, and especially dirt from the graves of your family and close friends is another subject all together. This kind of dirt is extensively used in hoodoo, which is an African American native magical practice. There are several books on Hoodoo, of which the best is, '*Hoodoo Herb And Root Magic*,' By Catherine Yronwode. Please note that hoodoo has no relation at all to Voodoo, which is actually a religion, just like Christianity or Judaism.

Burying An Enemy In The Earth

This spell makes use of the small wooden coffins that you can find in many Botanicas. Buy one of these coffins and try to buy a doll of the proper sex to fit inside it. If you wish to bury a man, you will need a male doll if you wish to bury a woman, a female doll. If these dolls are not available get a wooden clothespin, which you can mark a face on and dress with small pants for a man, or a dress for a woman. Now paint the coffin black on the outside, using black shoe polish if you wish. Line the inside of the coffin with paper, making it look as nice as possible. Now baptize the doll or clothespin, using the name of the person you wish to bury in the earth. Talk to the doll or clothespin, just as you would talk to the person, for example, you might tell it why you are going to bury it, explaining yourself and giving all of your reasons. Identify the doll or clothespin with the person as much as you possibly can.

When you are ready, tell the doll or clothespin that it is time for them to be buried. Put the doll or clothespin in the coffin and seal the lid shut. Gluing the lid with airplane glue is usually more satisfactory than trying to pin in closed with straight pins. If you glue the coffin, you must now wait for the glue to dry. Take the finished coffin to a cemetery, preferably an old one, and digging a hole, bury it. Avoid burying it in or on top of a present grave. It is best to burry it off to the side, in the overgrown bush area found in most old cemeteries. Once the coffin is buried, just leave it.

This spell does not kill people. Putting someone in the earth usually gives the person a strong desire to acquire the 'things of the earth.' These are always material things, which the person will suddenly become interested in acquiring, often spending far beyond their means to do so.

CHAPTER ELEVEN

Using Your Eyes Effectively

It is said that malochia, or the evil eye, is the result of beams of jealousy and envy coming from the eye of the envious one to that which is not pleasing to them. Malochia, one of the truly evil unconscious curses found on this earth, is just one thing that testifies to the power of the eyes. The seductive power of the eyes in flirting is another example of the power inherent in the eyes, and in the glance.

Of the senses, the eyes are one of the volitional senses, like the sense of touch of the hands. The eyes are under the conscious control of the mind, and see only where they are directed to look. The ears on the other hand, are an unconscious sense, as they are the unconscious receptors of whatever sounds are made within the range of hearing of the listener. We can use our eyes as a directed means of learning things we desire to know. Our ears simply inform us, concerning those sounds that are present in our enviroment, making no distinction as to whether we might wish to hear them or not.

In our society, one of the tests of the truth speaking person is that they look you directly in the eye when they are speaking to you. In other cultures, this is not so. Spanish speaking women almost never look a man directly in the eye, as in their culture, this behavior is thought to be provocative and sexually enticing. A Spanish-speaking woman who looked a man directly in the eyes might be considered by him to have loose morals. While this is a difference between cultures, looking other people directly in the eye can occasionally cause you some physical difficulty.

Avoiding Malochia And Negative Influence

Malochia is a curse that is usually transmitted from the eyes of one person to another. A person is at most danger for receiving malochia from another person when they are looking them directly in the eye. Many people attempt to influence others by sending them thoughts through the 'beams of their eyes.' They form a thought, and transmit it though their eyes to the eyes of the person they intend to receive it. Regardless of your belief in either Malochia or the influence of the eyes in transmitting thoughts, there is a simple method for preventing such negative influence from harming you.

Form the habit of looking at people by looking at the bridge of their nose, directly between their eyes. When you look at anyone, look at him or her there. Do not try to stare the person down, simply look at them in this way. They will be unable to see that you are not looking at their eyes, and at the same time, they will be unable to send you either Malochia or any other negative influence with their eyes.

Many people who have been afflicted by seemingly random headaches have found relief by practicing this simple technique. I suggest that you adopt it in your own life. This is one of those precautions that I believe is certainly worth taking. It may or may not be of conscious benefit to you.

Taking Control Of Conversational Groups

When you are in a conversation with a number of people, three or more, especially with people who are trying to convince you to their way of thinking, look directly at the person who is speaking. Then as that person pauses in their speech, look at another member of the group, as if you were expecting them to speak. Continue looking at that person passively, while mentally encouraging them to speak. Do not glance back at the first speaker, even if they resume speaking. Once the conversation begins following your glance, you have taken command of it, and you may now direct it as you wish.

Once you understand how to do this, you will find that it is easy to take control of conversing groups, guiding the group's conversation as you wish. This seeming miracle is accomplished using your eyes as the focus of an unspoken command. You simply begin by looking at the person you wish to speak next, shifting your eyes to them, from looking at the previous speaker. This means that you have been looking at, and mentally focusing all of your attention on the previous speaker. Now you are moving the focus of your attention, as well as your eyes, to the next person you wish to hear from. If you are sufficiently focused on the speaker, you will find that the conversation will follow as you direct with your eyes. As with many other techniques, this one requires practice.

You will find that several other people practice this technique as well, and it is often quite difficult to switch the leadership of the conversation from them to yourself. However, you can make this change in the leadership of the conversation if they drop their focus for any reason.

You will also find that if there is an established leader in the conversation, such as the chairman of a committee, they will have a much easier time controlling the conversation by using their eyes to control the conversation than anyone who is in the general body of speakers will. You should initially practice this art in groups of people who are conversing together in more or less random clusters of social chitchat. Once you master this technique, you will discover that it is a powerful ally for you in leading the conversation of groups of all kinds. You can do this by only encouraging those who agree with you to speak.

The Argument-Breaking Glance

When you see two people who are arguing, or who are in a heated emotion driven discussion, look between them. Do not look at either of them, look only at the space between them. Now think of your eyes as cutting the emotional tension between them. You can break the bond of emotion in their discussion or argument with your eyes. This will often cause the argument or heated discussion to deescalate, and in some cases to cease altogether. This is another useful technique for working with conversational groups, but it implies that you are not one of the people involved in the argument.

If you are still involving yourself in participating in futile arguments, you will have to put an end to that habit before you can make the most effective use of these techniques.

19756653R00057

Made in the USA
Lexington, KY
05 January 2013